CONCRETE
CLUES

A Genetic Genealogy Cozy Mystery Book One

CHRISTINE BURKE

For my *cousin* Janet.

Who would have known? Another mystery solved!

Thank you for supporting me on my DNA journey and letting me be a part of yours.

Did you know that there are 14,493 unidentified deceased persons across the United States?

These people are fathers, mothers, sisters and brothers.

Our goal is to speak for them and get them all identified using Genetic Genealogy.

THANK YOU!

The proceeds from the purchase of this book help fund our iniative.

Each case costs approximately $7,500 to work using Genetic Genealogy.

CHRISTINE BURKE

Concrete Clues was inspired by an actual unidentified human remains case.

There are more to come.

Learn More!

Concrete Clues

A Genetic Genealogy Cozy Mystery
Book One

Christine Burke

Pony Tale Publishing

Contents

Chapter 1
The Call From Harborville

O livia Mason's desk was a battlefield. Stacks of papers towered over her. A laptop screened the secrets of genetic codes. DNA testing kits were scattered like confetti. Her desk lamp painted an amber halo around her, highlighting the determination etched on her face. The crime-solver's spirit, it seemed, didn't retire when she had left the force. It just found a new playground.

Work was her calling. It had consumed her since she could remember. An ace detective with an undying thirst for truth. For her, crime and justice weren't just fields of work; they were her playground. The games, however, had cost her personal connections.

Olivia never envisioned a white picket fence or a traditional fairy-tale ending. Her world didn't make room for conventional romance. Long nights were spent not on dates but chasing leads. Dangerous criminals replaced potential suitors. Yet, she didn't see it as a loss. Her pursuit of justice brought her comfort.

She liked the thought of solving crimes, lending a helping hand. It was the adrenaline, the breakthroughs, the satisfaction of closing a case, and making a difference, that got her out of bed every morning. But sitting there, amidst forensic tools, she wondered about the what-ifs of having someone to come home to. Someone who could understand the double-edged sword of her life. It was a longing she'd often dismissed but never entirely forgotten.

She craved a connection beyond her work, a partner who could understand her complexities and bring balance to her chaotic life. But just as her mind drifted off, the DNA analysis screen flashed a lead in a cold case. Her excitement sparked back. The thrill of the chase was just too addictive.

Her phone rang, slicing the stillness in her office. Picking up, she managed, "Olivia Mason speaking."

"Is this Olivia Mason, the renowned forensic genetic genealogist?" The voice was urgent, a seasoned detective on the other end. A sense of intrigue flickered in her voice, "Yes, speaking. How may I assist you?"

"Detective Thomas, Harborville Police Department, Florida. We've reopened a homicide case from 1961. An unidentified woman found at the harbor. We need your expertise," he disclosed the case in earnest.

Her intuition already started putting the pieces together. A woman found washed up on the beach, anchored to a concrete block. She felt the weight of the truth she was about to unravel. Her voice full of conviction, she responded, "Detective Thomas, I've got your back. Between myself and the DNA, we'll identify this woman. Send me what you have, and I'll start reviewing it."

Her assistant, Lilly, who had been quietly observing, asked, "Well, don't keep me in suspense." Olivia turned to her with a knowing smile. "We have a new case. A cold one from Harborville, Florida, involving an unidentified woman found in the water. Tied to a concrete block."

Lilly's face echoed Olivia's excitement. "I'm ready, Olivia. Let's dive into it together."

"We'll gather all the information, research the historical records, and send off the DNA sample," Olivia began to outline the plan. "But first, we're going to meet Detective Thomas in person to get a better sense of the case."

The curtain had been lifted. The mystery of Harborville called to them. Olivia was ready to breathe life back into this woman's forgotten story and deliver the closure that had eluded her for decades. With Lilly by her side, their quest for justice had just begun.

Chapter 2
The Mystery Of The Woman In The Water

The tires of the rental car crunched on gravel as Olivia and Lily pulled into the sun-drenched streets of Harborville, Florida. The seaside town was a gem, colorful buildings brimming with life under the tropical sky, palm trees rustling in the balmy breeze.

Harborville sparkled with tranquility as they unfolded from the car, seagulls squawking over the salt-kissed harbor. Freshly baked pastries beckoned from a nearby bakery, curling around their senses, vying with the salty ocean air.

A chorus of amiable chatter bounced around them as they wove through the friendly locals. Olivia grinned at the close-knit community around her, soaking in the warmth of shared smiles and easy conversations.

"Look at this," she said, pointing at a cobblestone lane lined with quaint shops. "You can practically taste the connection between everyone here."

"Oh yeah." Lily's smile hinted at agreement, her eyes catching the sunlight. "A sense of community that's not just seen but felt. It's rare and beautiful."

A tantalizing scent from a nearby restaurant lingered in the air, reeling them in with an invisible lure. Olivia's stomach responded with a growl, her chuckle echoing in the empty street. "What do you say we see what Harborville's culinary scene is like?"

Lily's eyes lit up in anticipation. "Absolutely. Let's find a hidden gem, a place that's as charming as this town."

Their search led them to Harborview Bistro, wedged between a sunny yellow bakery and a quirky boutique. With a chalkboard flaunting the day's specials, it oozed a comforting allure.

"Let's give it a shot." Olivia gestured towards the restaurant, a pleased smile playing on her lips. "It feels just right, don't you think?"

"Couldn't agree more," Lily replied, rubbing her hands together in anticipation. "With the harbor so close, I bet they have fantastic seafood."

The moment they stepped inside, a rustic charm washed over them, bathed in soft lighting. As they settled at a corner table, their eyes scanned over the promising menu.

"From local seafood to artisanal dishes, this place seems to embody the spirit of Harborville," Olivia observed, leaning back in her chair.

"And this grilled snapper," Lily noted, "it's making my mouth water already."

Sharing their orders with a friendly waitress, they looked out onto the bustling streets, both content and excited. Olivia sighed, her gaze lingering on Lily's contented expression. "Our work sure takes us to amazing places, doesn't it?"

"To new discoveries, unraveling mysteries, and savoring the joys of life." Lily lifted her glass in a toast, her smile reflecting Olivia's.

As they left the restaurant, the calmness of Harborville wrapped around them. At the police department, the hum of daily business was a stark contrast, ringing phones and quick footsteps marking the rhythm of justice.

They were met by Detective Thomas, a seasoned man with a graying beard and wise eyes. His warm smile was a welcoming beacon in the bustling chaos.

"Glad you made it," he extended his hand. "We've been awaiting your expertise."

Their handshake was firm, the smile shared, full of promises. "We're here to help. Harborville seems to be a town full of welcoming people."

Detective Thomas nodded. "Despite our size, we do have our mysteries. We believe your skills can help us crack this one."

"Can't wait to dive in, Detective. What can you tell us about this mystery woman from the harbor?" Olivia was all ears.

The atmosphere in the room changed as Detective Thomas began. "She was found on March 4, 1961, but she's remained nameless for over six decades."

"What do we know?" Lily asked, her voice steady.

"Not much, I'm afraid." Detective Thomas ran a hand over his weary face. "We have a sketch, no ID, no fingerprint match, and no hits in the CODIS database."

Studying the sketch, Olivia's mind was already running ahead. "Had genetic genealogy been considered?"

Detective Thomas, the seasoned local policeman, was nodding appreciatively at Olivia's intent. "We've done all we can from a conventional perspective, hence we sought your expertise. We're hopeful that your knowledge and the breakthroughs in genetic genealogy can finally assign a name to this woman, bringing some respite to her kin, if any."

The determination within Olivia grew. "We'll deploy all our re-sources, Detective. However, we'll need all available evidence – cloth-ing, personal effects, anything that could potentially carry DNA. We'll inspect the earlier tissue sample used for CODIS and evaluate if there's enough left. If not, we'll need to extract fresh samples."

The gratitude was palpable in the detective's response. "Absolutely, we'll share everything we have. We still have her clothing from the incident. Some biological samples collected during the original inves-tigation have also been preserved."

As the trio talked about the logistics of securing the evidence, Olivia was eager to begin. The mystery woman wasn't just a face in a sketch anymore. She was an enigma waiting to be decoded, a story waiting to be narrated.

Olivia added, "I'll need access to the local genealogy databases un-der law enforcement capacity as well. With advancements in genetic genealogy, we stand a better chance than ever before of identifying her family and subsequently, her."

Detective Thomas's trust in Olivia's abilities was evident in his response. "You'll have our complete support, Olivia. We've seen the impact of your work. We're hopeful."

The DNA results had not been sent off yet, so Olivia, Lily, and Detective Thomas gathered around a large table in the police de-partment's conference room. Surrounded by stacks of case files and evidence folders, they began to dig into the case the old-fashioned way. It was time to delve into the minutiae of the mystery woman's case, examining the initial report and the events of that fateful night.

As Detective Thomas opened the case file, he traced the early stages of the investigation with a finger. "The call came on a Saturday night, around 11:30 p.m.," he began. "The caller reported a body washed ashore. It was a particularly high tide that night, and the water had left its mark."

Olivia probed further. "Any evidence at the scene that could give insight into how she ended up in the water? Signs of struggle or foul play?"

Detective Thomas flipped through the case file pages, his brow furrowed in concentration. "The preliminary scene analysis didn't reveal any immediate signs of foul play. No visible injuries or indications of a struggle. But, a rope was found around her right leg, attached to a concrete block. It seemed that the tide had washed the woman's body ashore. Despite the weight of the concrete block, the buoyancy created by her deceased body was enough to float her to the shore. Later, the medical examiner determined the cause of death to be blunt force trauma."

"A murder," Lily chimed in. "Any estimates on how long she had been in the water before being found?"

Detective Thomas's eyes scanned the case file pages as he responded, "Based on the preliminary assessment, it's estimated that the woman had been in the water for at least 24 to 48 hours. The tides and currents had carried her body to that specific beach spot."

Olivia asked, her voice softer, "Coming across a scene like that must have been tough, especially at night. How did it impact you, Detective?"

He sighed, his gaze distant as he recollected the moment. "Finding a body is always hard, no matter the circumstances. But that night was particularly haunting – the darkness, the waves crashing against the shore. It felt like a silent plea for justice, a call for answers."

Lily reached out to touch Detective Thomas's hand, her eyes filled with concern. "We understand the weight of this case. We're here to support you and do everything possible to uncover the truth."

Detective Thomas smiled in gratitude. "Thank you. Your dedication and determination have been instrumental in getting us this far. Together, we'll bring justice to this woman and offer closure to her family."

Thomas then described the items found on the unidentified woman. "The rope was about six feet long, made of sturdy nylon material. It looked like a utility rope, its brand and specific color unknown, though it had an orange hue. The concrete block was typical grey, the kind used in most local building construction."

He then detailed the woman's clothing. "She was wearing a one-piece lime green Jantzen swimsuit, with a halter neckline and a moderate-cut leg. It even had the iconic Jantzen logo at the hip." Olivia noted that the distinctive style and color could provide a potential identification lead.

Next, Thomas described the jewelry. "She wore two bracelets, one silver and one gold, both delicate and ornately designed. The silver one had intricate filigree work, while the gold one featured a pattern of alternating links. Additionally, she wore a silver ring with a small gemstone, likely a birthstone or a keepsake."

He finished with the woman's hairstyle. "The woman had curly, chestnut hair, styled into a medium-length perm, which the medical examiner noted appeared to be recent."

The pieces of the puzzle lay scattered before them, waiting to be connected and lead them to the truth they sought. The team dove deeper into the case file over the next few hours, scrutinizing photographs, reading the autopsy report, analyzing witness statements, timelines, and potential leads that could help identify the woman.

After concluding the briefing, Olivia and Lily left the conference room, their minds abuzz with the weight of the case. As they navigated the bustling corridors of the police department, Olivia turned to Lily.

"We're lucky," she said, her voice resonating with anticipation. "The mystery of the woman in the water presents another incredible opportunity for us."

Lily responded, her enthusiasm matching Olivia's, "I couldn't agree more. This case allows us to make a difference for at least one person, to bring closure to a decades-old mystery."

Stepping outside the police department, bathed in the warm glow of the sun setting over Harborville, they felt a renewed sense of purpose. Olivia couldn't help but feel a surge of energy, the weight of the case a pressing reminder of their task. The charming streets of Harborville, their picturesque buildings, and friendly locals hid a labyrinth of untold stories and hidden truths.

"In larger towns, the noise and chaos often overshadow the hidden truths. But here, in Harborville, the silence amplifies the whispers of the past. We are tasked with breaking this silence, to bring justice to those who've been forgotten."

"We'll start with the evidence," Olivia declared, her voice confident. "The clothing she wore, the biological samples – the tangible parts of her story. They're the key to unlocking her identity."

Lily added, "And once we have those pieces, we'll immerse ourselves in genetic genealogy, tracing her lineage, connecting the dots. We won't stop until we've found her family."

Their conversation turned lighter as they strolled along the harbor, finding momentary respite from the intensity of the investigation. They joked about the oddity of dying in a swimsuit, and the possibility of the perpetrator intentionally dressing the victim post-mortem. Olivia and Lily ended the day, their hearts united in the mission that lay ahead.

Chapter 3
The DNA Difference

O livia and Lily's night dragged out longer than a winter in the Arctic. They laid in separate beds, each itching for the dawn. The meeting with the Harborville police had left them hungry for answers, and eager to start the day's work: collect the DNA sample, ship it to the lab, and wait. Patience was a virtue, but not one Olivia had ever really mastered.

Despite the dance of the numbers on the digital clock at her bedside, Olivia was wide awake. Her mind spun like a hamster wheel with the weight of the case. Finally, she threw off the covers and hit the shower, deciding to get a jump on the day.

In the next room, Lily found herself in a similar predicament. The prospect of that all-important DNA sample kept her brain buzzing. Admitting defeat to insomnia, she swung her legs over the bed and set about readying herself for the day.

A short while later, Olivia stood at the window, watching the dawn break. A knock on her door interrupted her thoughts, and in walked Lily, fully dressed, a smile teasing her lips.

"Sleepless too?" Lily asked, joining Olivia at the window. "Feels like this case is already living rent-free in our heads, doesn't it?"

Olivia nodded. "I'm ready to hit the ground running. Bring justice to Harborville, bring closure for this woman."

After grabbing breakfast at the inn, they stepped out into the cool morning air, their breath misting as they walked to the end of the pier. The beautiful town felt at odds with the grim reality of their work.

On the weathered bench of the fishing pier, they ate their breakfast. Lily set down her coffee and turned to Olivia. "What's eating at you? You've been quiet."

Olivia looked out at the horizon. "It's hard, you know? A new case, the emotional toll. Being back in Florida, where I grew up..." Olivia's voice trailed off.

Lily knew the story well. Olivia's mother, an O'Malley, not a Livingston, as she'd always thought. Her grandmother's affair. Olivia's own biological father a mystery. The fallout. The search for identity. It all fueled Olivia's passion for their work.

"I can only imagine how you handle it," Lily said softly. "The work we do is tough, but for you, it's personal. Every case must feel like opening a wound."

Olivia nodded, a small smile touching her lips. "It's worth it, though. The power of genetic genealogy to transform lives, illuminate hidden connections, and rewrite lost narratives... it's a tool like no other. Sure, it's a rollercoaster, but it feels like everything in my life led me to this path. My experience as a detective, as a sergeant, and my own DNA drama, it all feels predestined, like the universe pointed me here."

With renewed resolve, she continued, "Let's go. The police department and the DNA that will give us the identity of our Jane Doe await."

They wrapped up breakfast, left the pier, and made their way to the police department. The morning was warm, the breeze salty.

Before they knew it, they were stepping into the bustling Harborville police department. They checked in, navigated the corridors, and walked into the conference room where Detective Thomas was waiting, the hope in his eyes apparent. Olivia and Lily had the potential to answer the questions that had haunted Harborville for years. It was time to get to work.

Detective Thomas had tipped his hat with a grin. "Ladies, a pleasure as always. Chain of custody is all shipshape. Good luck with the processing."

Olivia had nodded, dotting the 'i' on the form with a flourish. "We'll keep you in the loop, Detective. Be seeing you."

The sun was high when they left the precinct, casting sharp shadows along the streets of Harborville. The package was a precious cargo, cradled in Olivia's hands as they threaded their way towards the post office.

The small office smelled of fresh paper and hot electronics. The clerk was a cheerful man, oblivious to the significant burden about to be placed in his care.

"I need this sent priority, please," Olivia had said, gently placing the package on the scale. She kept the details to herself; less chance for the parcel to be intercepted or misplaced if it wasn't drawing any attention.

"No problem, Ma'am. I'll make sure it's handled with care."

There was a quiet moment of tension as the shipping labels were applied. The package was more than just a piece of evidence - it was a beacon of hope. The answers to countless questions rested in that small box.

Then it was out of their hands. Into the vast machine of the postal service, heading towards the labs that would unravel its secrets.

As they left the post office, the tension in Olivia's shoulders relaxed. She looked at Lily, a flicker of a smile playing on her lips. "We've done our part, now we wait. Next stop, the crime scene. But first, food. I'm famished."

Lily nodded, her own stomach growling in agreement. "Sounds good to me."

Their phones pointed them to a cozy café just down the street. The scent of fresh coffee and baking bread was irresistible after their morning's work. They grabbed a table in the corner and took a few moments to just breathe. The race was paused, now was the time to refuel.

"Two sandwiches and your tomato soup, please," Olivia ordered, rubbing her temples to ward off a headache. Lily nodded in agreement, the promise of a hearty meal stirring her appetite.

The food was just what they needed, filling and comforting. As they ate, the stress and worries of the morning were momentarily forgotten. Olivia leaned back, patting her full stomach.

"Alright, let's hit that crime scene," she declared, standing up.

Walking to the beach where Jane Doe had been found felt like entering a time capsule. The wind whipped their hair around, the salty scent filling their nostrils as they approached the spot. Olivia could almost see the community as it was back then; the quaint stores and relaxed pace of life making a stark contrast to the violence that had occurred.

"We should speak to some of the locals," Olivia suggested as they walked. "The folks in those businesses over there may remember something useful. Or have heard some tales that could shed light on what happened here."

"Good idea," Lily agreed, peering over at the storefronts. "There's nothing quite like local gossip for digging up the past. Let's see what they have to say."

Chapter 4
Making Connections

History seeped from every worn-out brick and rickety door in the small town as Olivia and Lily tread carefully on their path, eager to unearth secrets the locals might share about the long-ago crime. They were tugged into an old pharmacy, the doorbell's muted jingle proclaiming their entrance.

"Good day," Olivia launched in without any preamble, respect in her voice. "We're after the truth about the lady who washed up here in '61. Did you happen to see anything odd?"

The elderly owner's eyes filled with long-forgotten sorrow as he leaned on the counter. "A dark day for Harborville that was. No, I didn't see anything unusual, but the whispers? They never stopped."

Lily's pen hovered above her notepad, ready to ensnare any vital clues. "Do you happen to have any souvenirs from that time?"

Nostalgia softened the man's gaze. "Let me get what I have."

While waiting, Olivia's gaze fell on the vintage pharmacy bottles, a vivid reminder of the town's rich history. The owner returned with a small box and gently set it on the counter, "Old photographs, newspaper clippings, my father's belongings."

Gratitude swelled within Olivia and Lily as they left the pharmacy, a box of precious artifacts in hand. These small remnants of the past felt heavy with significance, invaluable keys to understanding the mystery woman's story.

Hours spent on their feet, walking and knocking on doors, yielded a patchwork of memories, stories, and half-remembered details from the elderly locals. Mr. Jenkins, a curious mix of concern and curiosity, filled their notebooks with tales of Harborville in 1961.

"Harborville was a safe place, a close-knit community," he reminisced. "A crime like that? It shattered us."

"Can you recall anything about the businesses around that time?" Olivia pressed, pencil ready.

Mr. Jenkins smiled. "Rosie's Diner was the heart of the town. You should check out the grocery store and pharmacy too."

Their bones ached as they left Mr. Jenkins' home, their notebooks heavy with new leads. "I could do with a break. We've only got the grocery store left on our list for today," Olivia suggested, and Lily agreed with a relieved nod.

They wandered the grocery store aisles, choosing a makeshift dinner to take back to the hotel. Their conversation in the room was light and filled with laughter, a welcome respite from the heavy task of their investigation. Over a makeshift feast, Olivia raised her glass, "Here's to our progress and the road ahead."

Time slipped away from them as they finished their meal and tidied up their room, preparing for the next day. Olivia quickly jotted down the tasks for tomorrow, "Library, historical society, any other repositories."

Lily nodded, stifling a yawn. "We should hit the sack, Olivia. See you in the morning." Olivia echoed her sentiment. As Lily left for her room, Olivia paused to absorb the quiet solitude of her hotel room, already thinking about the next day's investigation.

The comfort of the hotel room beckoned her to rest, promising a few precious hours of tranquility before a new day began with fresh leads and new possibilities. The echoes of the day's encounters mingled with her thoughts, fueling her determination to uncover the truth of Harborville's mysterious past.

Chapter 5
Unraveling The Lime Green Clues

S unlight seeped through the hotel blinds, beckoning a fresh day. Olivia and Lilly made a swift raid on the breakfast bar, bringing back a haul to their room. As much as they relished the hotel comfort, they knew they couldn't ignore the growing pile of cases awaiting their attention back home. Today marked their return, and they'd tackle the remaining investigation digitally, a nod of gratitude to their tech-empowered era.

Olivia thumbed through the case file, her eyes hungrily devouring every detail. The ring of her phone pierced the silence, making them both jump. She answered with bated breath, her pulse quickening. "Olivia Mason on the line."

On the other end, the familiar voice of their regular lab technician chimed in, "Olivia, confirming receipt of the DNA sample. Analysis will start now. We'll send you the sequenced file when ready."

She hung up, a wave of relief washing over her, a smile dancing on her lips. She turned to Lilly, triumph lighting her face. "The lab has our sample. It's under analysis, the sequenced genome is just a matter of time now."

Lilly's face mirrored her excitement. "This is huge, Olivia. We're closer to unmasking the mystery."

Determined, Olivia's gaze dropped to their digital investigation portal on her laptop screen. "There's a lot to do yet. Once we receive the sequenced file, we'll need to decode it, search for potential genetic matches, and build the family tree for our Jane Doe."

"We won't give up," Lilly affirmed, crossing her arms. "This woman's identity is owed to her, her loved ones need closure."

Now aware that their DNA sample was under analysis, they turned their attention to Harborville's history, visiting the library and the historical society. They dug into town records, perused newspaper archives, and unearthed family histories from online articles. In 1961, Harborville was a town on the cusp of change, its nostalgic charm giving way to modernization.

They learned about the revered Harborville Art Festival, a beloved annual event that united the town in music, food, and art. But it was this festival that had been tarnished by the discovery of Jane Doe's body, both occurring on the same day.

With each uncovered fragment of Harborville's past, they felt an ever-strengthening bond with the town and its people. Every conversation, every shared memory inched them closer to understanding the tragic events of that fateful year.

With time ticking away, they turned their focus to physical evidence. "Let's start with the most peculiar piece—the victim's bathing suit. We need to turn over every stone."

Lilly nodded, her laser-like focus on the task at hand. "The swimsuit is unusual, indeed. We need to inspect it, from fabric to design. It could shed light on our Jane Doe's mental state or even lead us to her killer."

The bathing suit, with its bright hue and unique pattern, held a promise to unlock the Harborville mystery. Olivia dived into historical records and set up interviews with locals who could provide insights on the fashion trends of that time.

As they toiled together, encircled by piles of documents, Olivia allowed her mind to wander back to her childhood memories linked to Alco bathing suits. She stood up, stretched, and shared her nostalgia with Lilly.

"Lily, my grandma used to own Alco bathing suits. They were a style statement back then, made her feel confident and glamorous."

"Really? Now you've got me picturing my own grandma in one of these," Lily quipped.

"I'm serious, Lilly. Alco swimsuits held an allure for their quality and timeless designs. My grandma loved them, and that's why I've always had a soft spot for Alco."

Lily grimaced. "I'm just glad we're dealing with a Alco swimsuit, not those antiquated bathing caps. Imagine trying to solve a case wearing one of those!"

The lighthearted moment passed as Olivia refocused on their mission. They needed to track down the people who might remember the swimsuit's origins, a crucial step towards Jane Doe's identity.

"We need to cover a lot of ground," Olivia declared, "We'll contact locals who might recall the fashion of that era. If we can trace the swimsuit's origins, we might be closer to knowing who this woman was."

They plunged back into their online investigation, searching historical archives, reaching out to locals via phone and email. They spoke to ex-boutique owners, fashion enthusiasts, and longtime Harborville residents, each contact drawing them closer to the swimsuit's origins.

As they had to drive to the airport, they packed up their gear, checked out of the hotel, and set off. As they got into the rental car, they looked back on Harborville, its charm and their memories intertwined, their hearts aflutter with a blend of achievement and excitement for the path ahead.

"We've made some significant strides in our investigation, got to know the community, and unraveled a part of the mystery," Olivia noted, adjusting the rearview mirror. "But it's time for us to head home."

"Harborville will always be close to our hearts," Lilly agreed. "The people, their stories, our progress—they will continue to inspire us. But we have more to do. It's time we took this back to our HQ."

Their departure from Harborville wasn't a farewell, rather a pause. They carried the town's memories, its connections, and their new-found knowledge with them, a tangible link to Jane Doe and her story.

On the plane, Olivia and Lilly poured over the story of the lime green Alco swimsuit. A local sensation in the summer of 1960, sold in a now-defunct boutique, it had swept the town's women off their feet. They uncovered photos and anecdotes that painted a vivid picture of that era. The swimsuit had become a symbol of freedom and carefree spirit.

Their conversations with Harborville's older residents revealed stories of beach parties, laughter, and a thriving community spirit during those summers. The lime green swimsuit, they realized, held a story of its own, a story interwoven with the people who had worn it. Their task was now to trace its journey, from creation to its tragic end on Jane Doe's lifeless body.

Chapter 6
The Two
Surgical Scars

T he next day, barely off the plane and back into work, Olivia and Lily hit pause on their non-stop sleuthing. They opted for a detour to the nail salon for a bout of relaxation. Excitement danced in their eyes. They were in dire need of some downtime, and today, pampering was the name of the game.

Inside the salon, soft tunes whispered through the air. Lavender oils and citrusy scents wrapped around them. Lounging side by side, they scanned the rainbow of nail polish shades. Lily's fingers landed on a vivid lime green.

"Going green today," she declared, flashing a playful grin at Olivia. "A shout-out to our Harborville puzzle."

A ripple of laughter escaped Olivia. "Saluting the case with a color. We're stirring intrigue, right at our fingertips."

The duo leaned back into their chairs, allowing the salon experts to work their magic. A symphony of nail files and polish brushes filled the air. Olivia eyed Lily's lime green nails. A brainwave hit her.

"This case's signature shade," she suggested, nudging Lily. "Our nail color could be our secret handshake, our badge of honor for cracking the case."

"Like a neon beacon of justice," Lily chimed in, amusement crinkling her eyes. "Our lime green war paint!"

Relaxation made way for a sober thought, pulling Olivia back to the heart of their mission. "This case," she mused, glancing at Lily, "is just one amongst thousands. So many nameless victims wait for their stories to come to light."

A grave nod from Lily. "Last count was over 14,000. That's an ocean of untold tales. Real people, lost in time."

"Feels like we're fighting against the tide," Olivia murmured, frustration edging her voice.

"But we've got the tools to turn the tide," Lily countered. "We could give these cases the attention they need. Maybe through a public awareness campaign, or partnering with groups fighting the same fight."

An idea sparked in Olivia's mind. "Books. We could write about these cases. Give each one a spotlight. Show the world their humanity, their dreams, their unknown stories."

Lily's eyes lit up. "Yes! We could tug at readers' heartstrings. Connect them to these lost souls. A book has that power."

The concept of a podcast followed. "A podcast could amplify our efforts," Olivia added. "Bringing these cases to life. Offering expert insights, interviews, behind-the-scenes peeks into our investigative process. We could call it Unknown Humans Remain."

Lily bubbled with excitement, a chastising glance from the nail technician barely dampening her spirit. "I love it! Our stories, reaching thousands, straight to their ears. An engagement platform for listeners. A chance to offer leads, participate in identification. We could bridge the gap between these forgotten souls and the world."

Nodding together, they let the potential of their idea sink in. Their mission was about to get a whole new dimension.

Olivia rummaged for her notebook, already planning their next moves. "We can start with the oldest, forgotten cases. Document them, podcast about them. We'll give each story the attention it needs. Let's get these unknown humans known."

Lily buzzed, itching to get her hands dirty. "We'll light these cases up with deep research and expert connections. Our books and podcast will peel back the layers of the unknown, giving closure to grieving families."

Green nails glinting in the sunlight, Olivia and Lily got back into the car, feeling refreshed and rejuvenated. The bold polish color was a reminder of their mission, and the fun, unexpected moments they found amidst it.

At the office, they continued investigating the mystery swimsuit, diving into old records and retold tales. They traced the life of the lime green swimsuit, from fabric and thread in a distant factory, to its last moments on the unidentified woman.

But the deeper they went, the more convoluted it became. The swimsuit's story was slippery, like water slipping through fingers. Olivia and Lily, however, didn't scare easy. They knew mysteries were often tangled webs of dead ends and distractions. They broadened their search, considering new perspectives, looking for hidden ties to guide them through.

Next up? The mystery woman's body. These scars were potential treasure troves of information, they could help identify their victim.

Squinting at Olivia's laptop screen, the duo studied the McBurney and Pfannenstiel scars. "These scars could lead us to her," Olivia said, "We find someone who had an appendectomy and a cesarean section, and we find our woman."

Lily squirmed in her seat. "Sounds easier said than done, HIPPA regulations aside. But on the bright side, we aren't looking through piles of medical records. Let's just hope this is the right prescription."

Their search led them to doctors, obstetricians, hospitals, and general practitioners. Harborville wasn't too big, thankfully. Olivia and Lily started reaching out, compiling medical histories. Women who'd undergone both surgeries, women doctors had lost touch with. Their list grew.

"Our woman is dead. That much we know." Olivia stared at the screen, eyes locked on their list. "These scars are common. We're likely to find many who fit our profile. Each one needs a thorough look."

Lily sighed. "What if none of these women are her? What if this leads us to a dead end?" She cringed at her unintended pun.

Days turned into a maze of frustration and determination as they ran out of leads. They reached out to local support groups, to medical professionals, to online communities, expanding their search.

By the week's end, Olivia frowned at their lack of progress. "We've found dozens of women with scars. None match. It's like searching for a needle in a haystack."

"We thought these scars would lead us straight to her. But it's proving more difficult than we thought. What if we've hit a wall?" Lily looked drained.

Olivia paused, then spoke firmly. "This is when genetic genealogy shines. DNA analysis and genealogical research can uncover connections traditional methods can't. It can give answers when all else fails." She glanced at Lily, a gleam in her eye, "And I believe our DNA results will be here soon."

Closing their office for the day, Lily left for a Scottish clan society meeting while Olivia opted for some leisure time. "Enjoy the Scottish get together!" Olivia called after her, "Can't wait to hear all about the kilts and tartans!"

"Thank you, Olivia. Have fun with whatever you have in mind!"

With mischievous excitement, Olivia thought of a new go-kart track that had caught her attention. The need for speed beckoned her.

Arriving at the track, vibrant sights and cheerful sounds surrounded her. Laughter and excitement filled the air as she made her way through the park. The twists and turns of the track ignited her adrenaline, and she surrendered herself to the carefree spirit of the moment.

The laughter of thrill-seekers blended with Olivia's own as she raced through the exhilarating course. The fast cars and the freedom from the investigation's weight brought her pure joy.

Leaving the amusement park, Olivia wore a contented smile. It had been a day of escape, a break from the rigors of their work. Though the Harborville mystery remained unsolved, she had claimed a well-deserved victory on the go-kart track. "Take that," she said, happily driving home to put herself—and the case—to bed.

Chapter 7
The Enigmatic Bracelets And Ring

B ack at work the next day, Olivia and Lily met up in the small kitchen. Their adventures from the previous day still filled their thoughts.

Lily's eyes sparkled with enthusiasm as she spoke first. "You won't believe the incredible time I had at the Scottish clan society meeting! People wearing traditional tartans, sharing stories, and celebrating our heritage—it was invigorating! I even learned a traditional dance called the Highland Fling."

Olivia grinned, knowing the significance of this experience for Lily. "That sounds amazing! I can imagine the vibrant atmosphere and the sense of community. Embracing your heritage and finding joy in it is truly wonderful."

Lily nodded, her excitement evident. "It was unforgettable. The sense of belonging and the passion for our cultural history were in-spiring. It reminded me how our heritage shapes our identities."

Unable to contain herself, Olivia burst out with her own tale. "Hold onto your seat! I had an adrenaline-filled adventure at the local amusement park. I raced around a go-kart track and won! The wind in my hair, the curves—it was like being a true champion!"

Lily smirked playfully. "You and your love for competition, especially in a go-kart. I can only imagine the speed and excitement. It must have been an absolute blast! Congratulations on your victory!"

Olivia beamed, pride evident in her expression. "Thank you, Lily! It was a fantastic way to embrace the joy of the present. Racing and feeling that rush—it reminded me of the thrill of living life to the fullest."

They laughed, momentarily escaping the weight of the investigation as they relished their personal achievements. Coffee and Diet Pepsi in hand, they returned to their desks.

Having exhausted leads with the surgical scars, they shifted their focus to the jewelry worn by the Jane Doe. Olivia meticulously examined the delicate bracelets and ornate ring while Lily looked into books and articles, searching for historical references.

Olivia's thoughts deepened as she studied the designs and craftsmanship. The intricate filigree work and gemstones hinted at a bygone era. Understanding the jewelry's context could unravel the mystery of the unidentified woman.

Excitement filled Olivia's voice as she spoke. "If this jewelry is hand-crafted, it tells a story. We need an expert in antique jewelry to decipher its hidden meaning. Someone who can shed light on its origin and significance."

Lily nodded, taking on the task. "I'll reach out to renowned antique jewelry experts and historians. Their insights into the time period and potential familial connections tied to these accessories could prove invaluable."

Olivia and Lily immersed themselves in the world of antique jewelry. They explored historical records, fashion magazines, and expert opinions. They interviewed specialists, examined photographs, and compared intricate details to known styles and trends.

A few days later, Lily entered Olivia's office with a sense of excitement. "I think I've found something. I came across an article by a renowned antique jewelry expert specializing in early 20th-century pieces. Her name is Isabella Rossi, and her bio is impressive."

Lily shared the details, her voice brimming with urgency. "Isabella Rossi is highly regarded, coming from a long line of jewelry artisans and gemstone enthusiasts. Her expertise spans art history, gemology, and jewelry forensics. She's known for her attention to detail and solving mysteries through analyzing jewelry."

Olivia's eyes lit up with anticipation. "We need to contact her immediately. Arrange a Zoom meeting or phone call. Time is of the essence."

Lily wasted no time and quickly made the necessary arrangements. Soon, they found themselves engrossed in a video call with Ms. Rossi, her vibrant voice and personal style shining through the screen. They eagerly shared photos of the jewelry, explaining its intricacies.

After a thoughtful pause, Ms. Rossi's voice reverberated with reverence. "These bracelets and the ring exhibit remarkable artistry. They belong to a distinct period in the early 1900s known for intricate metalwork called 'filigree.' Custom-made or acquired from reputable jewelers, such pieces were a symbol of affluence. Tiffany & Co. and Marcus & Co. were prominent jewelry houses during this time, but if the purchaser was a traveler, the Buccellati and Castellani families in Italy might have created them."

The possibilities opened up before them, and Olivia and Lily leaned in, eager to uncover the hidden stories within the jewelry.

Olivia's mind raced with newfound possibilities. The words of Ms. Rossi and the connections they had uncovered sparked a realization within her. "Could these accessories be a symbol of family heritage? Passed down through generations?"

Rossi nodded, confirming the possibility. "It's certainly possible. Jewelry often holds sentimental value and is passed down as heirlooms. Considering any familial connections tied to the unidentified woman is worth exploring. I would suggest delving into family histories, searching for photos, genealogical records, and perhaps reaching out to reputable antique dealers who might have insights into the origin of these pieces."

Thanking Rossi for her invaluable input, Olivia's mind brimmed with newfound possibilities. "Lily, we need to dig deeper into the family histories of the region. Find any potential connections to families known for their affluence during that time period. We might uncover a significant lead."

Lily nodded, already engrossed in her research. "I'll scour genealogical records, historical documents, and local archives. If there are any familial ties to these accessories, we will find them."

Like dogs on a bone, Olivia and Lily tirelessly combed through records, piecing together fragments of history. They interviewed elderly locals, traced family trees, and connected the dots. In their relentless pursuit of the truth, a particular family name caught Olivia's attention—The Andersons.

It was just an ordinary day, yet as they pursued their investigation, something clicked in Lily's head. Her eyes widened with a sudden realization. The name Anderson appeared in the local family histories they had been researching, as well as on the NamUs missing persons list—an Emily Anderson, a woman who had vanished years ago. Furthermore, one of the doctors had provided the name of an Emily Anderson, who should also bear the same type of scars—McBurney and Pfannenstiel—found on the unidentified woman.

"Olivia!" Lily's voice echoed from her office, brimming with a mix of excitement and disbelief. "It seems that Emily Anderson, listed in the NamUs missing person database, could be connected to the jewelry and the scars. Oh-my-goodness!"

Olivia quickly made her way to Lily's office, their paths crossing in the hallway. "That's incredible! It's starting to come together. The jewelry, the scars—it all points to Emily Anderson. But what could have happened to her? Why did she disappear?"

Lily's mind raced, contemplating the possibilities. "Okay, we need to delve deeper into Emily's life and uncover any connections she may have had to the unidentified woman. There must be a reason her presence and her scars match those of the unknown woman. We cannot ignore this significant piece of the puzzle."

Invigorated by the breakthrough, the women continued their investigation, shifting their focus to Emily Anderson's disappearance. They pored over old newspaper clippings, police reports, and reviewed statements from family members and friends who knew Emily. Every detail mattered as they searched for answers that would bridge the gap between Emily's disappearance and the unidentified woman found in the water.

They discovered that Emily had been a young woman with dreams and aspirations, beloved by her family and friends. But her sudden disappearance had left everyone baffled and grieving, a wound that had never truly healed.

One evening, Olivia and Lily were able to connect with Mrs. Johnson, an elderly relative of Emily's, who was willing to share a long-held family secret. They were eager to hear what she had to say.

Through the computer screen, they observed a frail figure in a worn-out armchair, assisted by her night nurse, Stan. Olivia began the conversation, her voice gentle yet filled with curiosity. "Thank you for meeting with us. We're hoping you can shed some light on Emily's disappearance."

Mrs. Johnson, her voice trembling with a mix of regret and relief, started to speak. "Emily was a vivacious and kind-hearted young woman. But she carried a secret burden, one that she thought she could bear alone. She had a child out of wedlock—a son. It was a different time back then, in the '60s, and Emily feared the judgment and shame it would bring."

Olivia nodded, her voice gentle yet eager. "Please know that we appreciate your willingness to speak with us. The police have been searching for Emily for quite some time, and any information you can provide would be immensely helpful."

Tears streamed down Mrs. Johnson's cheeks as she sighed. "I never intended to reveal this secret, but I can no longer bear the weight of it. Emily... she's not missing. She's alive and well. She's been living in Spokane under a different name, Janet Alexander."

Lily's eyes widened, her heart pounding with a mix of excitement and confusion. "Janet Alexander? Are you certain? How did she end up there?"

Mrs. Johnson nodded, her emotions pouring out. "Yes, Janet Alexander. It was a difficult decision for her to leave everything behind, including her family. She had been facing some challenges and needed a fresh start. Emily felt that assuming a new identity was the only way to find the peace and stability she yearned for. She swore me to secrecy, and now I'm violating her trust."

Olivia's voice was filled with empathy. "We understand that life can be overwhelming at times, but Emily's... uh, Janet's loved ones have been searching for her, worried sick. Is there any way we can contact her, let her know that her family cares and wants to reconnect?"

Mrs. Johnson hesitated, torn between loyalty to Emily's decision and the genuine concern of Olivia and Lily. "I can't give you her contact information. I've done enough by revealing her new name. Promise me, promise me that you'll be understanding and leave her alone. Janet has built a new life for herself, and she may not be ready to face her past just yet."

Olivia and Lily exchanged glances, understanding the delicate nature of the situation and the need to approach it with sensitivity. "We promise," they said in unison.

With gratitude, Mrs. Johnson thanked them, and the Zoom call came to an end. Olivia and Lily were left with a mix of emotions. Excitement pulsed through their veins, knowing that Emily, now Janet, was supposedly alive. Yet, they also understood the importance of respecting Janet's wishes and giving her the space to tell her story on her terms.

Olivia sighed, closing her laptop and gazing at the silent office space. "Another day of waiting. I can't help but feel impatient, Lily. The DNA results hold the key we've been searching for. Please, Lord, deliver us the DNA!"

Lily responded, her voice tinged with frustration. "I hear you. It's hard to be patient when we're so close to uncovering the truth. But we've done all we can for today. Let's close up the office and get some sleep. Tomorrow is another day."

They closed their laptops, gathered their belongings, and Olivia paused for a moment, her gaze lingering on the quiet office. "Okay, see you tomorrow." With a sigh, she locked the door, and both women left in their vehicles, yearning for peaceful and productive slumber.

Chapter 8
Digging Into The Genetic Code

The morning sun began to cast its gentle glow on the streets as Lily arrived at their office earlier than usual. Anticipation surged through her veins, jumpstarting their investigation. But as she approached the office, she spotted Olivia's car already parked in the lot, light spilling from the windows.

Curiosity ignited, Lily quickened her pace and entered the office to find Olivia engrossed in her work, eyes fixed on the computer screen. A smile tugged at Lily's lips, witnessing her punctual partner already hard at work.

Olivia's voice held surprise as she greeted Lily. "Lily, you're here early. I couldn't sleep, restless with the possibilities of today. I wanted to get a head start on the tasks."

Lily chuckled softly, admiring Olivia's unwavering dedication. "Well, that makes two of us, as usual. I couldn't sleep either. The excitement got the better of me."

Olivia's eyes lit up. "Well, good thing you did because... the DNA results are here!" Olivia's excitement spilled over, causing Lily to call out from the kitchen, "Don't you dare start without me!"

Both settled at the conference room table, their gazes fixed on the computer screens, a mix of anticipation and nerves bubbling inside them. They were ready to evaluate the biological relative matches, armed with fresh diet soda and coffee, prepared to delve into the genetic code and unravel the unidentified woman's identity.

Olivia began to evaluate the possibility that the Jane Doe could be Emily Anderson. Despite the elderly relative's words, they had no concrete proof. The jewelry found on the Jane Doe matched that of the Anderson family, and Emily, who disappeared years ago, bore the distinctive McBurney and Pfannenstiel scars. It seemed like a solid lead.

Meanwhile, Lily logged in to the DNA databases, peering into the biological relative matches of their Jane Doe, devising a game plan.

Olivia commenced constructing Emily Anderson's family tree, feeling a mixture of hope and dread. On a good note, if it wasn't Emily, it meant she was alive and not missing. But on a bad note, if it wasn't Emily, a promising lead would go up in smoke. Such was the nature of their work.

Utilizing the record repositories in Ancestry.com and FamilySear ch.org, as well as other member's family trees, Olivia swiftly crafted Emily's family tree. Technology's wonders had condensed what used to take months or years into mere minutes.

With the family tree completed, Olivia began sorting the top biological matches from Jane Doe, comparing them with the information gathered from Emily's genealogical family. The divergence between genealogy and genetics became increasingly frequent, a lesson Olivia had learned through her own experiences. Trusting the DNA was paramount. As Olivia often said, and with her future book title in mind, "DNA Doesn't Lie, But Your Momma Might Have!"

Disappointment began to creep in as Olivia's findings didn't align with the known relatives of Emily Anderson based on biological DNA. It became evident that the unidentified woman was not Emily. Mrs. Johnson had been telling the truth.

A pang of disappointment washed over Olivia. "Lily, it's not Emily Anderson. I had hoped to bring closure to her family, but it seems we've hit a dead end. However, we must press on. There are still other matches to explore, and we owe it to this unknown woman to find the truth."

Lily sighed empathetically, and they commenced assigning tasks, following Olivia's "roadmap," a curriculum she had taught to police and individuals, aiding them in finding persons of interest quickly and easily. It was a positive outcome stemming from Olivia's "DNA Drama, allowing Olivia to pay it forward.

Olivia and Lily redirected their attention to the emerging matches, meticulously examining each one, constructing family trees, tracing connections, and gathering information. Among the matches, a third cousin stood out, holding great promise.

Olivia's voice filled with anticipation as she shared her findings with Lily. "This third cousin match has a robust family tree spanning several generations. Their ancestors' locations align with this area. We're on the right track."

Lily leaned in closer, her eyes filled with curiosity. "What can we learn from this match, Olivia? How can we uncover the woman's identity?"

Olivia's fingers flew across the keyboard as she pulled up the details of the third cousin's family history. "By examining the shared DNA segments and cross-referencing with historical records, we can narrow

down the potential branch of the family tree that leads to the unidentified woman. It's like solving a complex puzzle."

They spent hours meticulously analyzing the matches, piecing together the woman's family tree. Geographical connections, historical
events, and ancestral migration patterns began to reveal clues.

As they explored the matches, certain family names stood out—relatives with strong ties to the Harborville community. Each match had
a unique story, shedding light on the woman's potential origins and
bringing them closer to the truth.

Jack Morrison, a descendant of the town's founding family, had
roots in Harborville dating back to the early 1800s. Olivia speculated
that the unidentified woman could have a direct connection to the
Morrison family.

Nancy Whitman, a lifelong resident and high school cheerleader
mentioned in news clippings from the 1930s, also caught their attention. Olivia and Lily examined Nancy's family tree, searching for
any overlapping branches that could lead them to the unidentified
woman.

Bobbi Reynolds, whose ancestors were renowned fishermen in
Harborville's thriving fishing industry, provided another potential
lead. Olivia wondered if the unknown woman had been part of this
tight-knit community, perhaps even involved in the fishing trade.

After an eventful morning of uncovering potential leads, Olivia and
Lily took a break to enjoy a well-deserved lunch at their favorite local
deli. As they sat at their table, they reminisced about their interactions
with the locals and how their lives intertwined with the relatives of the
Jane Doe.

Back at the office, the duo felt they were getting closer. Excitement
filled the air as Olivia and Lily began connecting the dots. Each match

represented a thread in the tapestry of the woman's identity, bringing them closer to unraveling her story.

Hours passed, and Olivia rubbed her temples, her eyes bleary from intense concentration. The room was cluttered with papers and the faint scent of caffeine. Lily let out a yawn, contemplating a brief nap right there. They had reached the point of genealogy delirium.

Olivia chuckled, her voice tinged with exhaustion. "You're right, Lily. I don't think my brain can handle any more DNA segments and shared centimorgans right now. We've done a fantastic job today, but it's time to call it a night."

They exchanged weary smiles, their exhaustion mingling with a sense of accomplishment. They knew a good night's sleep would bring a fresh perspective.

Lily stretched, the sound of her joints cracking breaking the silence. "Fresh eyes, fresh perspective, right?"

Olivia nodded, her eyelids growing heavier. "Sounds like a plan. Let's dive into the world of dreams and hope they hold the key to our next breakthrough."

With a final exchange of laughter, Olivia locked the door, knowing that the challenges of the case would be waiting for them in the morning. But for now, they embraced much-needed rest, confident that a new day would bring fresh clues and unexpected revelations to their investigation.

Chapter 9
Unearthing
Secrets

T he next day arrived, and Olivia and Lily dove into the meticulous examination of shared centimorgan ranges among their promising matches—Jack Morrison, Nancy Whitman, and Bobbi Reynolds. Their goal was to unearth clues about the unidentified woman's parentage. Hours of research and scrutinizing family trees revealed intriguing patterns within the DNA matches.

Olivia pointed excitedly at her computer screen. "Look at this. The shared centimorgans and the science behind it are revealing a clear truth. Based on the centimorgan ranges and our roadmap, there's no denying it. Our unknown deceased woman is the half-sibling of Thomas Morrison, a cousin of Jack Morrison, one of our highest matches!"

A triumphant smile illuminated Lily's face. "That's incredible!"

Olivia raised a hand, eager to share more. "But wait, there's more! The DNA measurements also confirm that our Doe is the half-sibling of Margaret Whitman, a cousin of Nancy Whitman, our second highest match. The puzzle pieces are falling into place!"

"Wow, wow, wow, wow!" Lily exclaimed, jumping up and down in excitement.

Olivia continued, "And here's the icing on the cake. The centi-morgan calculation shows that our Jane Doe is the niece of Robert Reynolds, who we know is the son of Bobbi Reynolds, another close match. We've connected the dots and uncovered the most recent common ancestors. Jane Doe is the daughter of John Morrison and Catherine Whitman."

"Woo, Hoo, Hoo!" Lily shouted, unable to contain her enthusiasm. "Wait, I'm still confused," she said, dejectedly. "How can our Jane be the daughter of John Morrison and Catherine Whitman? They were never married, and they were married to other people."

Olivia looked at Lily with a raised eyebrow and a smirk. "Ummmm, well, Lily, you've heard of the birds and the bees, right? It takes two to tango, so to speak, and it doesn't always require a marriage license. Remember what happened to me?"

Lily's eyes widened with realization. "Ooooooooooooh. So, Thomas and Margaret must share a parent."

Olivia corrected her, trying to conceal her exasperation. "No, Thomas and Margaret don't share a parent with each other. They only share Jane Doe. Jane is THEIR half-sister. These 'oopsies' happen more often than you know, Lily. I'm living proof! Our Jane Doe would be like me, a Not Parent Expected or 'NPE.' Sometimes it's called mis-attributed parentage or 'MPE'."

"O-M-G, I get it!" Lily exclaimed. "Sheesh, just like you always say, Olivia, DNA doesn't lie!"

Olivia continued, "Moving ahead, because Jane matches relatives on Mrs. Whitman's maternal side of the family, and not John Morrison's, Catherine Whitman has to be Jane's mom, which makes Margaret Whitman Jane Doe's half-sister. According to the records and fam-ily trees, Catherine only had two daughters, Margaret Whitman and Sarah Whitman."

"And last but certainly not least, Margaret is alive and well according to her Facebook page this morning, and Sarah is nowhere to be found. Ta-da! Our believed-to-be Jane Doe has to be Sarah Whitman."

Lily pumped her fist in the air, exhilaration coursing through her. "Yes! We did it, Olivia! This is a major breakthrough in our investigation. We've unveiled the intricate web of familial relationships, and it's going to lead us to the truth!"

Olivia laughed with elation, their shared excitement reverberating through the room. "Can you believe it? We've deciphered the genetic code, followed the centimorgan clues, and unraveled the mystery. It's moments like these that make all the hours of research worth it!"

Lily raised her hand for a high five. "To us, the genealogy detectives who cracked the case! We're one step closer to finding the truth and bringing closure to these families. Yippee!"

They smacked their hands together, celebrating their hard-earned success and the thrill of the breakthrough. The room buzzed with energy, the air filled with a sense of triumph and possibility. They knew there was still work ahead of them, but in that moment, they reveled in their achievement, savoring the joy of discovery.

Their conversation continued to brim with excitement as they eagerly discussed their next steps, mapping out the path forward. They recognized that while DNA never lies, solid genealogy supported their theories, along with a detailed report. They were ready to complete the identification armed with newfound knowledge and a renewed determination to uncover the full story. But first, they decided to treat themselves to a well-deserved celebratory lunch—they were famished.

Opting for Mexican food, Olivia and Lily headed to a local Cantina. The warm smile of the waitress greeted them as she handed them menus filled with an overwhelming number of options.

As they perused the menu, laughter and joy filled their conversation. The weight of the investigation momentarily lifted, replaced by the delight of a well-earned respite. They shared stories, exchanged jokes, and savored the camaraderie that had flourished between them.

When the waitress came to take their order, Olivia couldn't help but inquire about the restaurant's specialty. "Excuse me, we've heard rave reviews about the food here. Could you recommend some of your most popular dishes?"

The waitress's eyes sparkled with enthusiasm as she described the mouthwatering carne asada. "Our carne asada is a true crowd-pleaser. It's a juicy and flavorful grilled steak, marinated in a special blend of herbs and spices. Served with rice, beans, and warm tortillas, it's a dish that captures the essence of traditional Mexican flavors."

Olivia's mouth watered at the description. "That sounds incredible."

The waitress nodded; her voice filled with pride. "You won't be disappointed. It's one of our most popular dishes."

She then pointed to another option, eager to share her knowledge. "Now, let me tell you about our tamales. They're a cherished Mexican delicacy made with masa, a corn-based dough, filled with various savory or sweet fillings, and wrapped in corn husks before being steamed to perfection."

Olivia and Lily exchanged intrigued glances, eager to learn more. "What kinds of tamales do you offer?" Olivia asked.

The waitress smiled. "We have traditional pork tamales, filled with seasoned shredded pork. For those who prefer chicken, we offer mouthwatering chicken tamales, with tender, seasoned chicken enveloped in the masa. And if you're looking for something vegetarian, we have delicious cheese and jalapeño tamales. They have just the right amount of kick!"

Lily's eyes lit up with excitement. "We'll have to try a variety of tamales. They all sound incredible."

The waitress jotted down their order, matching their enthusiasm. "Excellent choices! You're in for a treat. I'll have that out to you in no time."

Olivia and Lily eagerly awaited their meal, their eyes wandering around the vibrant Mexican restaurant, taking in the colorful and eclectic decor that adorned the walls. Intricate papel picado banners hung gracefully from the ceiling, casting a warm glow over the dining area. Paintings depicting traditional Mexican scenes adorned the walls, transporting the patrons to distant lands filled with vibrant markets, bustling streets, and breathtaking landscapes.

Olivia's attention was captured by a large mural depicting the stunning beaches of Acapulco. Memories of her own travels to the coastal paradise flooded her mind. Turning to Lily, she asked, "Have you ever been to Mexico, Lily?"

Lily shook her head, curious. "Not yet, Olivia. But it's definitely on my travel bucket list. I've always been fascinated by the rich culture, stunning landscapes, and, of course, the mouthwatering cuisine."

Olivia smiled, reminiscing. "Mexico is truly remarkable. I've been fortunate enough to visit Acapulco, Mexico City, Guadalajara, and Cancun. Each city has its own unique charm and attractions."

Lily leaned in, captivated. "Tell me about Acapulco. I've heard it's a paradise with beautiful beaches."

Olivia's eyes gleamed with fondness. "Indeed, Acapulco is a tropical paradise. The pristine sandy beaches, framed by majestic cliffs, are simply breathtaking. I remember soaking up the sun, lounging by the azure waters, and witnessing the mesmerizing cliff divers perform their daring acrobatics. It was unforgettable."

Lily nodded, imagination whisking her away. "And what about Mexico City and Guadalajara?"

Olivia's voice held a nostalgic tone. "Mexico City is a bustling metropolis teeming with history and culture. The vibrant streets are filled with ancient ruins, magnificent architecture, and vibrant markets offering an array of handmade crafts. As for Guadalajara, it's known for its rich traditions, beautiful plazas, and the lively mariachi music that fills the air. Exploring the colonial streets and sampling the cuisine were highlights of my visit."

When the food finally arrived, the tantalizing aroma filled the air, teasing their senses. They dug in, savoring each bite.

As they indulged in the feast before them, conversation flowed effortlessly. The weight of the investigation lifted, replaced by the simple joy of good food, friendship, and shared accomplishments. They relished the moment, allowing themselves to revel in the well-deserved respite.

Between mouthfuls of delectable food, Olivia raised her glass, gratitude shining in her eyes. "To us, Lily! To our unwavering determination, our tireless pursuit of the truth, and the bonds we've forged along the way. Cheers!"

Lily's glass met Olivia's with a resounding clink. "Cheers, Olivia! We've come so far, and we're not done yet. Here's to finishing what we started and bringing closure to those who seek answers. And of course, to fantastic food!"

Chapter 10
Sharing
Secrets

L ater, still stuffed to the gills, Olivia and Lily found themselves
back in the office, surrounded by stacks of papers and family
trees. Their tireless research and analysis of the shared centimorgan
ranges among Jack Morrison, Nancy Whitman, and Bobbi Reynolds
had led them to a breakthrough. Anticipation filled the room as Olivia
began to share the backstory.

"I believe the woman's parentage points to a complicated time,"
Olivia started, pulling out a folder containing army records. "According to these records, Catherine Whitman, Margaret's mother, was
married at the time of our Jane Doe's conception. However, during
that period, Mr. Whitman was overseas serving in the military."

Lily's brows furrowed as realization dawned. "So, you're saying the
Jane Doe, er...Sarah must be the product of an affair?"

Olivia nodded, confirming Lily's understanding. "It seems likely.
Considering the timing and Mr. Whitman's absence, the evidence
strongly suggests that Catherine had an affair during that time, result-
ing in the birth of the woman we've been investigating."

Re-reviewing the shared centimorgan ranges, Olivia and Lily were
confident that Thomas Morrison was the unidentified woman's

half-brother, Margaret Whitman was her half-sister, and Robert Reynolds was her uncle. The centimorgan mix provided a crucial link between the characters, unveiling the truth about the unidentified woman's familial connections within Harborville.

The weight of the revelation hung in the air as Olivia and Lily absorbed the implications of their findings. The complexity of the family's history was unraveling, revealing a tale of secrets and hidden connections. Their research had unearthed a truth that had long remained hidden, shedding light on the tangled web of relationships and providing a deeper understanding of the woman's origins. However, there was still a missing piece of the puzzle—Sarah Whitman's DNA details remained unknown to her newfound half-family.

With Thomas Morrison as the half-sibling of the lady in question, the ladies researched the background of his father, John Morrison. Olivia searched online for answers about John Morrison's life. "Look at this. John Morrison was quite the intriguing character. From what I've gathered, he was known for his charisma and adventurous spirit."

Lily raised an eyebrow, intrigued. "Oh, really? That could shed some light on why he may have had an affair. Restless nature and a craving for new experiences could explain his actions."

Olivia nodded, her face filled with thought. "Exactly. It's possible that John Morrison felt confined within his marriage, yearning for excitement and a sense of freedom that he couldn't find within his existing relationship."

Lily leaned back, contemplating the possibilities. "You know, sometimes people seek out extramarital affairs as a way to fulfill their unmet needs or to escape the routine of their daily lives. It's not an excuse, of course, but understanding his character might help us unravel the motives behind his actions."

Olivia sighed, her voice tinged with empathy. "Marriages can be complicated. Perhaps John Morrison found himself yearning for something different, something that ignited his sense of adventure. It's unfortunate that he chose to pursue an affair, but we have to consider the circumstances that may have led him down that path."

Lily nodded, her gaze distant. "Indeed. Relationships are intricate, and it's important to delve into the depths of people's motivations to truly comprehend their actions. By examining the people and exploring their desires, we can gain a better understanding of the dynamics at play."

With renewed determination, Olivia turned back to the screen, ready to dive deeper into the other connections. "Let's keep digging."

Olivia's mind wandered as she considered the circumstances surrounding Catherine Whitman, Margaret's mother. "Lily, I think we need to explore the challenges that Catherine and Mr. Whitman faced during his military service. The emotional toll of war can put immense strain on relationships."

Lily nodded, her expression filled with empathy. "Absolutely. The prolonged absence and uncertainties of war can create a difficult situation for families. When my John was gone on his Med cruises, it was awful. With all the kids to take care of myself, I understand how Catherine might have felt lonely and overwhelmed during that time."

Olivia sighed, her voice filled with understanding. "War takes a toll not only on those serving but also on their loved ones back home. The emotional burden and the constant worry can push individuals to seek companionship and emotional support in unexpected ways."

Lily's eyes filled with compassion. "Catherine may have found herself yearning for connection and support amidst the hardships she faced. The affair could have been a way for her to cope with the challenges of separation and the emotional turmoil that war brings."

The room fell into a contemplative silence as Olivia and Lily acknowledged the complexities of Catherine's situation.

Olivia leaned back in her chair, her voice filled with a mix of fascination and empathy. "Can you imagine the weight Catherine must have carried, keeping this secret all these years? It must have been a profound internal struggle for her."

Lily nodded, a pensive expression on her face. "Indeed. Catherine's circumstances during that time were undoubtedly challenging. With her husband overseas, she may have longed for companionship and emotional support. The affair could have been a result of seeking solace amidst the chaos of war."

Olivia reached for a worn photograph from a stack of documents, her fingers tracing the image. "I wonder how Catherine's path intertwined with that of John Morrison. Was it a fleeting connection or something deeper?"

Lily contemplated the possibilities. "It's difficult to say. We may never know the full story or the motivations behind their choices. But it's clear that Catherine's decision to present the woman as a Whitman was an act of protection, shielding her child from the harsh realities of societal judgment and preserving the family's reputation."

As they continued their discussion, Olivia and Lily were reminded of the complexities of human relationships. Each discovery they made deepened their understanding of the interconnected lives and the intricate tapestry of family history. They also knew it was time to seek further assistance in solving this family mystery.

With their evidence neatly organized, Olivia picked up the phone and dialed the number of Detective Thomas, the seasoned police detective assigned to the case. After a few rings, he answered, his voice confident and professional.

"Detective Thomas speaking," he said.

"Detective, it's Olivia," Olivia greeted. "I have some compelling findings that shed light on the unidentified woman's identification. We think we've identified her, and we believe it's crucial to pursue further interviews with any surviving biological family members. Can we arrange a Zoom meeting to discuss our discoveries?"

Detective Thomas listened attentively, his curiosity piqued. "Absolutely, Olivia. Wow, that's such great news. Do you have time to do it this afternoon? We'll review your findings and devise a plan for interviewing the biological family."

Relief washed over Olivia as she thanked the detective. She hung up and turned to Lily, excitement gleaming in her eyes. "Lily, this is it. We have a chance to dig even deeper and bring closure to the family. Please schedule a Zoom call for today at 4 p.m. to present our research to Detective Thomas and lay the groundwork for connecting with the surviving biological relatives."

Lily nodded, sharing in Olivia's enthusiasm. "Our findings are solid, and with the detective's support, we can navigate through any legal hurdles and sensitively approach the potential family members. We owe it to the woman and her descendants to uncover the truth. I'll email you the link."

The hours ticked by as Olivia and Lily prepared their research, gathering the documentation that would strengthen their case. Later, at the meeting time, they started the call.

Detective Thomas came on, his demeanor welcoming yet focused. Together, Olivia and Lily showcased family trees, revealed the science behind centimorgans, demonstrated the applicable centimorgan ranges, and reviewed other evidence. The detective absorbed the information, his brow furrowed as his mind processed the intricate connections.

Detective Thomas sat straight in his chair; his eyes focused on his computer screen as he searched his databases looking for Sarah Whitman. Olivia and Lily sat on the edge of their seats, their anticipation palpable in their office. They had presented their findings to Detective Thomas, explaining their belief that Sarah Whitman was their Jane Doe, and now they anxiously awaited his discoveries.

As the keyboard clacked beneath his fingers, Detective Thomas nodded to himself, deep in concentration. He found something, revealing a report filed by a Mr. Nels from nearby Sandy Shores police. He told them to wait while he printed it out. His eyes widened as he read the details.

Olivia couldn't contain her excitement any longer. "Detective Thomas, tell us!"

He looked up at them, a mix of surprise and satisfaction evident in his expression. "You won't believe this. Sarah Whitman was indeed reported missing in 1961, but not here in Harborville."

Lily's eyes widened, a mixture of relief and astonishment washing over her. "So, Sarah was reported missing, but not in the same place where our Jane Doe was found. That's why we couldn't find the match earlier."

Detective Thomas nodded, his voice filled with understanding. "Exactly. The discrepancy in the location and the timing of the report made it difficult to establish the connection. The entry made by Sandy Shores police didn't include the specific details about scars and distinguishing features, so the match was not immediately apparent. The report was filed in Sandy Shores by a Mr. Nels. It says he was her boss. One thing weird though, Sarah was reported missing on March 20, 1961. We found our Jane Doe on March 4, 1961. There's got to be an error here. Are you sure that Jane Doe is Sarah Whitman?"

Olivia exchanged a glance with Lily, a mixture of uncertainty and conviction in her eyes. She took a deep breath, her voice steady but filled with determination. "Detective Thomas, I understand the discrepancy in the dates raises some questions. However, the DNA evidence we have is compelling. The genetic genealogy matches and the centimorgan ranges all point to a strong likelihood that our Jane Doe is indeed Sarah Whitman. We've spent countless hours meticulously analyzing the data, and the results consistently lead us to this conclusion."

Lily nodded in agreement, her voice echoing Olivia's confidence. "The DNA doesn't lie, Detective. We understand that the timing doesn't align perfectly with the reported missing date, but there may be factors we're not yet aware of. Our focus now should be on gathering additional information and exploring any leads that can help us establish a concrete connection."

Detective Thomas studied the determined expressions on their faces, a mix of curiosity and trust in their eyes. He nodded slowly, acknowledging their conviction. "I admire your dedication and the extensive work you've put into this investigation. It's clear that you believe in the DNA evidence and its significance. We'll need to look deeper into the circumstances surrounding the reported missing date and explore any other possibilities. We owe it to Sarah Whitman and Jane Doe and their families to uncover the truth."

Olivia let out a sigh of relief, her voice tinged with excitement. "But now that we know Sarah was reported missing, it all starts to make sense. The pieces of the puzzle are finally coming together."

Detective Thomas continued. "We still have some work to do to verify this information and establish the concrete link, but your research and findings have opened up a promising lead. It seems as if we are closer than ever to uncovering the truth."

Lily's heart raced with anticipation. "Detective Thomas, what's our next step? How do we move forward from here?"

Detective Thomas leaned back in his chair, his gaze steady. "First, I need to let the Chief and my Lieutenant know what you've uncovered. Then, I need to confirm the details of Sarah's missing person report and gather any additional information. I'll reach out to the Sandy Shores police department and request their records."

Olivia nodded, her voice filled with determination. "We're ready to assist in any way we can, Detective. This breakthrough has given us renewed energy to see this through to the end."

"This is compelling indeed," Detective Thomas remarked, his voice laced with intrigue. "While we wait for the reports from Sandy Shores, I think it's important to schedule interviews with the surviving biological family members. Let's work together to approach this delicately, ensuring we respect their privacy and emotions while seeking the truth, especially because they may not be aware of the real biological relationships. I suggest you meet with them alone, trying to get general background information until we later confront them with the biological truth."

Olivia and Lily nodded in agreement, appreciating the detective's sensitivity and dedication to the case. Olivia agreed, "We'll get back to Harborville as soon as we can. It's late, and we can look at travel arrangements tomorrow and send you the details."

Detective Thomas thanked them and left the online meeting. With their collaboration solidified, Olivia and Lily were ready to return to Harborville. They were eager to contact the identified family members, each step bringing them closer to unraveling the hidden secrets and granting closure to the woman's lineage.

Chapter 11
Missed Opportunities

Olivia and Lily's subsequent return to Harborville filled them with a mix of anticipation and excitement. They boarded their flight, ready to embark on another chapter of their investigation. As fate would have it, their journey included a long layover in Dallas, providing them with an opportunity to indulge in a delicious meal once again.

Seated in a lively airport restaurant, Olivia and Lily found themselves amidst the savory aromas of slow-smoked meats and tangy BBQ sauces. The tantalizing scents wafting through the air awakened their taste buds, reminding them of the flavorful delights they had savored during their previous visit to Harborville.

Menu in hand, their eyes widened with anticipation. "How about we indulge in some authentic Texas BBQ during our layover?" Olivia suggested, her voice filled with excitement.

Lily's face lit up with delight. "Absolutely, Olivia! Texas is renowned for its mouthwatering BBQ, and we can't miss this opportunity to experience it firsthand."

They ordered a variety of smoked meats—brisket, ribs, and pulled pork—each prepared with meticulous care and served with a side of traditional BBQ accompaniments. The plates arrived, a colorful spread of smoky goodness that had been crafted with passion and expertise.

As they took their first bites, the tender meat melted in their mouths, infused with layers of smoky flavor and complemented by the tangy-sweet BBQ sauce. The side dishes of coleslaw, cornbread, and pickles added delightful contrasts of texture and taste.

Olivia savored a succulent bite of brisket and exclaimed, "This is incredible! The slow cooking process has created such tender and flavorful meat. It's no wonder Texas BBQ has such a legendary reputation."

Lily nodded in agreement, wiping a dribble of sauce from her chin. "I couldn't agree more, Olivia. The smoky aroma, the perfectly caramelized crust, and the explosion of flavors—it's a true BBQ masterpiece."

As they relished their BBQ feast, Olivia and Lily engaged in conversation, discussing their plans for the upcoming investigation in Harborville. They revisited their previous encounters, reminiscing about the people they had met, the leads they had uncovered, and the mysteries that still awaited resolution.

Lily straightened the napkin in her lap and said, "I have a feeling this trip back to Harborville will lead us to significant breakthroughs. We've already made connections with the local community, and with our continued efforts, I believe we're getting closer to unraveling the truth behind Sarah our Jane Doe."

Olivia nodded, her gaze focused. "You're absolutely right. The pieces are coming together, and with each step, we're gaining momentum."

Their layover came to an end, and Olivia and Lily left the restaurant, their taste buds satisfied and their spirits lifted. The flavors of the BBQ lingered, infusing them with a renewed sense of purpose. Boarding their connecting flight, they settled into their seats, eager to once again immerse themselves in the enigmatic world of Harborville, fueled by the lingering essence of authentic Texas BBQ.

Arriving in Harborville, Olivia and Lily checked into their familiar hotel. When they randomly received the same rooms as last time, a sense of serendipity washed over them. It seemed that the universe was aligning the pieces of their investigation, offering subtle signs that they were on the right path. They couldn't help but embrace the mystical world of numerology and universal coincidences, finding intrigue and comfort in the hidden connections that permeated throughout their lives and their cases.

As they settled into their rooms, Olivia noticed the recurring presence of the number seven in her room number. It had been the same during their previous stay. She smiled, recalling the significance of the number in numerology—a symbol of introspection, intuition, and spiritual growth. It was as if the universe was gently reminding her to trust her instincts and delve deeper into the mysteries that lay ahead.

In Lily's room, the number three appeared prominently. It had been the same during their previous visit as well. Lily couldn't help but feel a sense of joy and optimism, as the number three was often associated with creativity, communication, and the power of collaboration. It was a reassuring reminder that their partnership held a significant role in unraveling the secrets of Harborville.

Before getting settled for the night, Olivia and Lily engaged in spirited conversations about the power of numbers and the hidden messages they may hold. They mused over the interconnectedness of their experiences, finding comfort in the belief that the universe was conspiring to guide them towards the truth.

As they prepared to embark on another day of unraveling the mysteries of Harborville, Olivia and Lily couldn't help but feel a sense of alignment with the universe. The recurring numbers in their hotel rooms became talismans of hope and guidance, grounding them in the belief that their pursuit of truth was not just a matter of chance, but an orchestrated dance between the seen and the unseen.

With hearts open to the hidden messages that surrounded them, Olivia and Lily each drifted off to a peaceful slumber, the sound of the waves crashing along the shore keeping them company.

The next morning, bright-eyed and bushy-haired due to the humidity, Olivia and Lily reviewed the background on the recently identified Jane Doe, Sarah Whitman, and her biological family. They sat on the hotel room sofa, surrounded by stacks of research materials and old photographs they had gathered online and from their previous visit. The conversation turned to Sarah Whitman "aka Jane Doe," an unbeknownst talented artist whose life they were observing now on display.

Olivia held a printout of a black-and-white photograph of Sarah, her eyes studying the captured image. "Look at her. Sarah Whitman was undeniably a remarkable woman. Her artistic talent shines through her every feature."

Lily nodded, a wistful smile on her face. "You can see the passion in her eyes and the vibrant energy emanating from her smile. She must have been such a life force in the town of Harborville."

Olivia's voice was filled with reverence as she continued, "Sarah's curly chestnut hair adds to her unique and artistic aura. I can only imagine the inspiration and creativity that flowed through her veins."

Lily read through a biography, captivated by the portrait of Sarah's life. "Between the ages of 40 and 50, Sarah would have been at the peak of her artistic prowess. Decades of honing her craft, expressing herself through her artwork, and leaving a lasting impact on the community."

Olivia set the photograph down gently, a mix of admiration and sadness in her eyes. "It's heartbreaking to think that Sarah's life was cut short. She had so much more to give to the world, so many more stories to tell through her art."

Lily nodded in agreement, her voice filled with determination. "That's why it's crucial for us to honor Sarah's memory and uncover the truth about her family. By shedding light on her lineage, we're not only piecing together her story but also ensuring that her legacy lives on."

Next, their focus came to Catherine Whitman, Sarah's mother, and her background in Harborville. They had uncovered intriguing details about Catherine's involvement in the community, but there were still questions surrounding her actions regarding Sarah's disappearance.

Olivia frowned, contemplating their findings. "Catherine Whitman was highly regarded in Harborville. She was deeply involved in the arts community and played a significant role in promoting local artists. Our research shows that after Mr. Whitman was killed in the war, Catherine moved away from Harborville."

Lily's eyes widened, her voice filled with anticipation. "So, Catherine left town. What else did you find?"

Olivia's voice was steady as she continued. "According to local historical archives and eyewitness accounts, Catherine relocated to St. Pete, where she struggled with her grief and turned to alcohol as a means of escape."

Lily nodded, absorbing the information. "That would explain her absence from the community and her failure to report Sarah missing. Grief and addiction can cloud one's judgment and hinder their ability to fulfill their responsibilities."

Olivia reached for a weathered newspaper clipping and read aloud. "Here's an article reporting Catherine's premature death due to alcohol-related complications. It confirms our suspicions."

A mixture of empathy and sadness washed over Lily's face. "Poor Catherine. She must have been battling her own demons while trying to navigate the overwhelming pain of losing her husband. It's tragic how her circumstances affected her ability to be there for Sarah."

Olivia's voice grew softer, reflecting their newfound understanding. "Yes, it is tragic. Our research has shed light on the complex and heartbreaking journey Catherine went through. It helps us understand the reasons behind her actions or lack thereof during Sarah's disappearance."

Lily looked to Olivia. "Now that we know Catherine's story, we can approach Sarah's surviving relatives with compassion and a deeper understanding of the challenges Catherine faced. It's important to remember that they, too, have been shaped by these circumstances."

"Absolutely, Lily. Our research has given us the key to unlocking the truth. With this newfound knowledge, we can piece together the puzzle of Sarah's disappearance and hopefully bring some closure to her family and this case."

With appointments scheduled for the next day, they sought out something fun and something to take their mind off the case. Olivia and Lily found themselves aboard a picturesque paddleboat dinner cruise, gliding along the shimmering waters of Tampa Bay. The warm evening breeze tousled their hair as they took in the breathtaking views of the bay's expansive coastline, dotted with palm trees swaying gently in the wind. The twinkling lights of the city skyline created a mesmerizing backdrop against the darkening sky, casting an enchanting aura over the scene.

As they strolled along the deck, Olivia and Lily marveled at the beauty of their surroundings. Olivia couldn't help but express her admiration. "Tampa Bay is truly a captivating place. The combination of natural beauty and vibrant city life is awe-inspiring."

Lily nodded in agreement, a sense of tranquility washing over her. "You've got that right. The bay area offers a perfect blend of stunning coastal landscapes and a bustling urban atmosphere. It's no wonder people are drawn to this region."

Their conversation ebbed and flowed, mirroring the gentle movement of the boat. Olivia leaned against the railing, her gaze fixed on the distant lights. "It's moments like these that remind me why we do what we do. The beauty of this place, the stories waiting to be uncovered, and the hope of bringing closure to those affected by these mysteries—for me, it combines everything about me, what I like to do, and what gives me purpose."

Lily nodded, her eyes glimmering with a mix of passion and empathy. "Yes, that's it. Our work goes beyond just solving cases. It's about giving a voice to the voiceless, bringing answers to those in search of closure, and making a difference in people's lives. It's a calling we can't ignore."

As they continued their conversation, their attention turned to the delectable aromas wafting from the boat's dining area. The tantalizing scents of freshly prepared seafood and savory dishes filled the air, teasing their appetites.

Olivia sniffed mischievously. "I can't wait to see what's on the menu. It's not every day we get to enjoy a dinner cruise like this."

Lily chuckled, her eyes sparkling with anticipation. "Yes ma'am. It's good to take a moment to appreciate the simple pleasures life has to offer."

As the evening progressed, Olivia and Lily found themselves immersed in the magic of the Tampa Bay area, their hearts filled with gratitude for the opportunity to work together, explore the mysteries that surrounded them, and experience the beauty of the world around them. The paddleboat dinner cruise served as a reminder of the moments of respite and joy that could be found amidst their investigative endeavors, adding a touch of enchantment to their journey.

As the boat glided gracefully through the calm waters, and docked, they disembarked and walked to their hotel, enjoying the breeze and the moonlight up above. Despite being energized about the case, the duo was still tired from their travels and decided to make an early night of it. They knew they had both a busy and emotional day tomorrow. Praying for good fortune and as much good news as possible, they turned in and quickly fell asleep.

Chapter 12
Distant
Memories

T he next morning, armed with curiosity and a seemingly inno-
cent agenda, Olivia and Lily sat across the table from Margaret
Whitman, sister of Sarah Whitman, a renowned artist of yesteryears.
The room buzzed with anticipation as Margaret, oblivious to their
true intentions, prepared to share the story of her own artistic journey
and the legacy she had inherited from her beloved sister, Sarah.

Olivia dived right in, her eyes wide with feigned admiration. "Margaret, we've heard so much about your illustrious career as an artist.
We're dying to learn about the vibrant art scene that thrived in this
city back in the day. You and Sarah left quite an impression on the art
world, and we want to know the secrets behind your success."

Margaret chuckled, clearly flattered. "Well, it feels like a lifetime ago,
but I guess I can spill a few details about those glory days."

Lily jumped in, her voice filled with curiosity. "Margaret, your art
has always had a unique and captivating quality. How did you develop
your distinctive style? Did it come naturally to you?"

Margaret's eyes twinkled with nostalgia. "You know, it all started
with our mother, Catherine. She was the driving force behind our

artistic endeavors. She nurtured our talent and encouraged us to push boundaries."

Olivia, playing her part, probed further. "And what was it like growing up in Harborville, surrounded by the beauty of the ocean and the artistic community?"

Margaret's face softened, a wistful smile playing on her lips. "Harborville was a dream come true for us. We spent endless hours sketching by the shore, capturing the essence of our surroundings. Our mother made sure we soaked up the inspiration that this place had to offer."

Lily tilted her head, curiosity brimming. "Margaret, your sister, Sarah, is also an artist, right? How did her artistry compare to yours?"

Margaret's eyes glowed with pride. "Oh, Sarah was a force of nature. Her talent was extraordinary, and she brought a whole new dimension to our artistic endeavors. We were a dynamic duo, pushing each other to new heights."

Olivia seized the opportunity, injecting a touch of intrigue. "And what about your father? We've heard rumors of a tragedy that befell your family. Care to share?"

Margaret's expression shifted, a shadow crossing her features. "Yes, our father, Frank Whitman... He served in the war and never returned. It was a devastating loss for us. We had to leave Harborville, seeking a fresh start."

Lily's voice softened with empathy. "That must have been tough, Margaret. How did the move impact your artistic journey?"

Margaret let out a sigh, her eyes reflecting a mix of resilience and sorrow. "It was a turning point for both Sarah and me. We embraced the change, discovering new artistic communities in St. Petersburg. We found inspiration in the museums, galleries, and the people we met along the way."

"Are you and Sarah still close?" Olivia asked, her eyes fixed on Margaret, waiting for her response.

Margaret's eyes filled with sadness and longing, her voice carrying a hint of nostalgia. "The truth is, Sarah's disappeared... it's been years since we've had any contact. It never gets any easier, you know? It's been over 40 years, and the pain still lingers. After she vanished, everything changed. The uncertainty, the unanswered questions... it hurt me, emotionally and physically. I don't even know what to believe anymore."

Lily cautiously ventured further, her heart racing with anticipation. "Margaret, that's devastating news. We're truly sorry to hear that. Forgive us for prying, but when Sarah disappeared, were there any clues or events that stood out to you? Anything that might shed some light on what happened?"

Margaret's brows furrowed, her eyes clouded with a mix of sorrow and uncertainty. "Sarah's disappearance... it was a crushing blow. I've searched tirelessly for answers, but the truth remains elusive. There were whispers, rumors floating around, but nothing concrete. It's haunted me all these years, never letting go."

Olivia probed further, her concern evident in her voice. "What do you mean by whispers and rumors? That's truly awful!" Margaret's face turned solemn as she recounted the events, unaware of the hidden depths that Olivia and Lily were exploring. She raised a hand to her face, her voice tinged with worry and confusion.

"It was a few months before she vanished," Margaret began. "Sarah had just taken on a new position as the manager of an art gallery in a town about an hour away. She was so excited about the opportunity, and we were all thrilled for her. But then... I received a call from the gallery owner, a man named Mr. Nels." Olivia and Lily exchanged a brief glance when Mr. Nels's name was mentioned.

Margaret's voice trembled slightly as she continued, her eyes searching for answers that remained elusive. "Mr. Nels informed me that Sarah hadn't shown up for work on the Monday after the grand gallery opening gala. He was concerned because it was unlike her to miss work without notice. I was devastated, worried sick. I'll never forget that date. It was March 20th, 1961."

Olivia and Lily exchanged another significant glance, their hearts sinking as they realized the extent of Margaret's unawareness of Sarah's tragic fate. They listened intently, hoping to glean any information that might shed light on the circumstances surrounding Sarah's disappearance and help untangle the timeline.

Margaret continued, her brow furrowed, concern etched on her face. "I tried calling Sarah's home, but it just rang and rang with no answer. I reached out to the local authorities, but without any solid leads, there was little they could do at that point. It felt like a nightmare, not knowing where my sister was, not knowing if she was safe."

Olivia's voice softened, carefully chosen words delivering empathy. "Margaret, we understand how incredibly difficult this must have been for you. We want to help you find answers and bring closure. Are you okay with that? Can you recall anything else about that period? Did Sarah mention any conflicts or concerns before she disappeared?"

Margaret shook her head, tears welling up in her eyes. "I would appreciate any help you can provide. But honestly, there's nothing more. Sarah was so thrilled about the new gallery, so passionate about her work. She loved the art world, connecting with fellow artists. I can't fathom what could have happened. Why she might have run off like that."

As the conversation flowed, Olivia and Lily skillfully masked their true intentions, listening intently for any hints or slip-ups that might uncover the truth behind Sarah's disappearance. Margaret's words painted a vivid picture of their childhood and their artistic bond, but there were still missing pieces to the puzzle.

Olivia, with a hint of empathy, gently probed further. "Margaret, it must have been incredibly difficult for you when Sarah disappeared. Were there any clues or events leading up to her vanishing that stood out to you?"

Margaret's face clouded with sadness, her voice tinged with a touch of regret. "Sarah's disappearance... It shattered my world. I've searched for answers for years, but it's like chasing a ghost. There were whispers, suspicions, but nothing concrete. It haunts me to this day."

Lily leaned forward, her eyes sparkling with determination. "Margaret, we're here to help. We want to uncover the truth, to bring closure to Sarah's memory and to your lingering questions. If there's anything you can remember, any detail that might help, please share."

Margaret's shoulders slumped, a mix of grief and hope in her eyes. "Thank you. It's been a lonely journey. If there's anything I can do to assist, any piece of information that might shed light on what happened to Sarah, please let me know."

Olivia and Lily thanked Margaret for her willingness to cooperate, promising to keep her updated on their progress. They left the meeting with a renewed determination to delve deeper into the mystery surrounding Sarah's disappearance.

As they drove back to the hotel, Olivia and Lily exchanged a knowing glance, their minds racing with possibilities. The conversation with Margaret had unveiled fragments of the truth, but it had also deepened the enigma surrounding Sarah's fate. They knew that their investigation was far from over, and they were ready to face the twists and turns that awaited them on their quest for justice.

Chapter 13
Last Goodbyes

After their conversation with Margaret, Olivia and Lily knew they needed to speak with Mr. Nels, the art gallery owner and the last person to see Sarah. They researched him online, obtained his number, and arranged to visit him later in the day.

Mr. Nels resided in a quaint, two-story house tucked away in a quiet neighborhood. The exterior boasted a well-maintained garden with bursts of colorful flowers, while a white picket fence added a touch of charm. Inside, the house exuded warmth and nostalgia, with antique furniture gracing the living room and walls adorned with artwork that showcased his love for the arts.

Nels himself was a lean, elderly man with a neatly trimmed white beard that framed his weathered face. Though slightly dimmed by the passage of time, his eyes held a glimmer of the passion that had driven him in his younger years. His hands, adorned with a few age spots, betrayed a lifetime of handling delicate artwork and curating exhibitions.

Olivia and Lily settled into Mr. Nels' cozy living room, their eyes wandering around, taking in the carefully curated space. The air smelled musty, like aged books and faint hints of oil paint, creating an ambiance that embraced the artistic spirit.

After the initial pleasantries, Olivia engaged Mr. Nels in casual small talk to establish rapport and delve into his involvement with the gallery. Not wanting to pry too deeply just yet, Olivia and Lily skillfully steered the conversation toward the present, trying to uncover any hints or clues that Mr. Nels might unknowingly reveal.

Olivia looked directly at Mr. Nels, her eyes sparkling with curiosity. "We're intrigued by your connection to the art world. How did you first become involved with the gallery? It must have been quite a journey."

Mr. Nels chuckled, a twinkle in his eye. "Ah, yes. It feels like a lifetime ago. I've always had an appreciation for art, you see. When the previous owner of the gallery decided to retire, I saw an opportunity to channel my passion into something meaningful. So, I took over, determined to nurture local talent and share their creations with the world."

Olivia took a deep but silent breath, her voice gentle as she probed further. "Mr. Nels, we've been researching Sarah Whitman's disappearance. I understand you reported her missing? We're also trying to understand the impact it had on the gallery. Were there any challenges or changes that arose during that time?"

Lily joined in, her voice filled with genuine interest. "And how did things unfold after Sarah's disappearance? It must have been quite a shock to the gallery and the art community."

Mr. Nels' expression softened, a trace of sadness flickering across his face. "It was a devastating blow, I must admit. The gallery lost its guiding light, and the art community mourned the absence of such a promising talent. We reported Sarah's disappearance to the authorities, but as the days turned into weeks, hope dwindled. It was a difficult time for everyone involved."

Olivia and Lily exchanged empathetic glances, their hearts heavy with the weight of the unresolved mystery. They realized that beneath the friendly demeanor and the shared grief, there might be hidden truths yet to be uncovered.

As they sat across from Mr. Nels, their eyes fixed on him as they prepared to dig deeper into the last time he had seen Sarah. They wanted to gauge his reaction, searching for any hint of unease or suspicious behavior.

Olivia posed a question, her tone polite yet probing. "Mr. Nels, we're trying to piece together the events leading up to Sarah's disappearance. Can you walk us through the last time you saw her? Were there any details or incidents that struck you as odd?"

Mr. Nels adjusted his glasses, his face a mask of mild concern. "Of course, I'll do my best to remember. It was a long time ago. Let's see, it was after our gallery closed for the night. We had our first gala that evening, March 17th, to celebrate the grand opening. I remember the date because it was St. Patrick's Day and we had a themed party. Sarah and I were tidying up, discussing the success of the recent exhibition. She seemed excited about some new artists we were considering for future shows."

Lily studied Mr. Nels' demeanor, searching for any signs of discomfort. "And did anything stand out to you during that evening? Any peculiar interactions or strange occurrences that might have raised suspicions?"

Mr. Nels paused, his eyes searching their faces for a moment before answering. "To be honest, there was nothing concrete that I could pinpoint. However, looking back, there were a few instances when Sarah seemed preoccupied, as if she had something on her mind. But we all have our worries, don't we?"

Nels hesitated for a moment, his gaze shifting as if lost in thought, and added. "Well, there was nothing particularly out of the ordinary. Sarah was her usual self, enthusiastic and dedicated to her work. But I suppose there was one thing that struck me as a bit off. When I left the gallery that night, I noticed a car parked nearby that I didn't recognize. It seemed out of place for that time of night."

Olivia and Lily exchanged a glance, their curiosity piqued. "Do you remember anything about the car, Mr. Nels? Any distinguishing features or details?"

He furrowed his brow, straining to recall the details. "It was a dark-colored sedan, quite unremarkable, really. I couldn't make out the license plate, unfortunately. It might not be relevant, but it did strike me as odd at the time. I'm sure if you talk to the police, they may have more details. They took a report."

Olivia felt the need to probe more, her voice filled with anticipation. "We appreciate your recollection. Every detail could potentially be important. Can you tell us more about the timing? When did you notice the car parked nearby? And did you see anyone near it?"

Nels put a hand to his chin, his eyes distant as he retraced his memory. "It was just as we were closing up for the night. Sarah and I were the last ones in the gallery. I remember looking out the window and seeing the car parked on the street. It was about fifteen minutes past midnight. As for anyone near the car, I couldn't say for sure. It was dark, and I didn't see anyone nearby. But it did raise some suspicion."

Lily leaned in, her voice filled with curiosity. "Mr. Nels, did you mention this car or your observations to Sarah? Did she seem concerned, or did she mention anything about it?"

He shook his head, a hint of regret in his expression. "No, I didn't bring it up to Sarah. At the time, I didn't think much of it, just an odd occurrence. And Sarah was in her usual cheerful state, focused on her work. I didn't want to alarm her unnecessarily."

Olivia and Lily continued their questioning, seeking additional information about Mr. Nels' report to the police and whether he had any suspicions about potential suspects. He appeared cooperative, providing details about his interactions with the authorities and expressing his desire to assist in any way he could.

As the conversation drew to a close, Olivia thanked him for his time and cooperation, concealing their underlying suspicions. "We appreciate your time and willingness to share your recollections, Mr. Nels. Rest assured, we're committed to finding the truth behind Sarah's disappearance. If anything else comes to mind, please don't hesitate to reach out."

Nels nodded, his smile somewhat strained. "Thank you both for your interest in her case. Sarah was a remarkable young woman, and it pains me that her fate remains unresolved. I hope you can bring some closure to this heartbreaking situation."

Expressing their gratitude for his time and cooperation, Olivia and Lily bid Mr. Nels farewell. As they made their way back to their car, they reflected on the conversation, dissecting every word and gesture.

Lily broke the silence, her voice tinged with both determination and caution. "It's clear that Mr. Nels is holding something back. There's a sense of discomfort and avoidance in his responses. He is clearly telling us that Sarah was present in the gallery for the event on Friday, March 17th, but we know that Jane Doe, aka Sarah, washed ashore on March 4th. We need to continue our investigation, gather more evidence, and find the missing pieces of the puzzle. Let's start with learning more about that gala at the gallery."

Olivia nodded, her gaze focused on the busy street. She had a strong gut feeling that there was no way Sarah was at the gallery that night. She had full confidence in the DNA evidence. "You're right, Lily. We have to dig deeper, uncover the truth. We'll follow every lead, explore every possibility until we bring justice to Sarah and closure to all those affected by her disappearance."

"Let's stop off at the library to see what we can find on the gallery and the gala," Lily said.

With renewed determination, Olivia and Lily set off to gather more information, their minds already racing with the next steps in their quest for the truth. The dates were starting to reveal discrepancies, and they knew that untangling the web of events would be essential to uncovering the secrets that lay hidden in Sarah's mysterious disappearance.

Chapter 14
Painting The Picture

O livia and Lily sat side by side at a corner table in the local library, laptops open, digging through archives. The click of keys and the scent of old books filled the air as they searched for clues about the art gallery's gala. Excitement surged through them when Lily discovered an article that made their hearts race.

"Look at this!" Lily exclaimed, her eyes widening. "The gala made headlines. 'What Lies Beneath' sold for a whopping one million dollars! The buyer was Avery Randolph, and he's still here in town."

Olivia's curiosity sparked. "That's a lead we can't ignore. Let's find out more about Avery Randolph and what he knows about that night."

With newfound information, Olivia and Lily closed their laptops, their determination palpable. They exchanged a knowing look, silently agreeing on their next move.

They left the library, stopping at the Panera drive-thru for a quick lunch. Olivia, always efficient, devoured her chicken salad sandwich in the car, while Lily struggled to balance her soup in its bread bowl. Olivia couldn't resist a sarcastic remark. "Lily, just because it's a bowl, it doesn't mean it's made for the car." This resulted in a sheepish look from Lilly but did not deter her from eating.

Once satisfied and ready to face their next challenge, Olivia and Lily made their way to Avery Randolph's address. They approached an impressive house by the shore, marveling at its grandeur.

Olivia glanced at Lily, excitement bubbling inside her. "This must be the place. Let's gather information, but we need to be cautious. We don't know what we're getting into."

Lily surveyed the imposing structure. "We'll proceed with caution, follow our instincts, and expect the unexpected."

They rang the doorbell, their hearts pounding. The door swung open, revealing a distinguished man with silver hair and a welcoming smile.

"Good afternoon, may I help you?" Mr. Randolph inquired, politely curious.

Olivia took charge, her voice warm and inviting. "Mr. Randolph, I'm Olivia Mason, and this is Lily, my assistant. We're investigating events related to the Brightman Art Gallery's gala in 1961. We're particularly interested in your experience that night."

Recognition flickered across Mr. Randolph's face. "Ah, the gala and 'What Lies Beneath.' Please, come in."

Entering the grand foyer, Olivia and Lily admired the artwork adorning the walls. They followed Mr. Randolph to a cozy sitting room and settled into plush furniture. Their gaze was drawn to the captivating painting above the mantle, an exquisite depiction of marine life.

Mr. Randolph turned to Olivia and Lily, pride in his voice. "This is 'What Lies Beneath,' the highlight of the gala. Created by the renowned artist Winston Hauten, it's a masterpiece that brings the marine world to life."

Olivia's eyes sparkled with excitement, while Lily's curiosity deepened. "Winston Hauten? His work is highly sought after. The painting drew quite the attention. Can you tell us more about that night and your interactions with Sarah, the gallery manager?"

A hint of sadness crossed Mr. Randolph's face. "Unfortunately, Sarah wasn't at the gala. Many were disappointed, especially me. I was looking forward to seeing her there."

Olivia and Lily exchanged a knowing glance. There was a contradiction between Mr. Randolph's statement and what they had learned. Their curiosity grew, and Olivia pressed further.

"If Sarah wasn't at the gala, do you know where she was during that time?" Olivia inquired.

Avery furrowed his brow, searching his memory. "She had to leave unexpectedly. Mr. Nels told us she had to take care of her ill mother out of town. It was quite sudden."

Olivia's mind raced, trying to reconcile the discrepancies. "Mr. Randolph, we have information that suggests Sarah was at the Gala. Is it possible that you were supposed to meet her on a different date?"

Avery's smile faded slightly as he pondered Olivia's question. "I apologize for any confusion. Yes, we were supposed to meet on my birthday, March 6th. But she didn't show up, and I assumed she had other commitments. I followed up with Mr. Nels to verify the painting's provenance before purchasing it on the night of the gala. That's when I found out Sarah was gone."

March 6th? Olivia's gut twisted. It was around the same time Jane Doe washed ashore.

Olivia and Lily exchanged a significant look. Avery's account contradicted Mr. Nels' statement. They were on the verge of uncovering something crucial.

With a polite smile, Olivia thanked Mr. Randolph. "We appreciate your time, Mr. Randolph. If you remember anything else about that night or have further recollections, please don't hesitate to contact us."

As they walked back to their car, Olivia and Lily couldn't contain their excitement. The puzzle pieces were falling into place, and they were determined to find the missing link in Sarah's disappearance.

Lily's voice brimmed with anticipation. "Something's not right. Mr. Randolph's statement contradicts Mr. Nels'. Sarah wasn't at the gala because she was in the morgue! And why did Mr. Nels claim she left to care for her sick mother? Oh my gosh, Olivia... Catherine Whitman died from alcoholism the year before. Remember?"

Olivia's eyes widened, a surge of realization coursing through her. "You're right, Lily. We need to dig deeper, retrace Sarah's steps. There's a connection we're missing, and we won't stop until we find it."

With renewed determination, Olivia and Lily embarked on the next phase of their investigation. They knew that uncovering the truth meant unraveling the secrets and inconsistencies surrounding Sarah's disappearance.

Chapter 15
Beach Party

O livia and Lily armed themselves with a list of names from the society reports, ready to interview the workers and artists who attended the public grand opening and the employee's only luau celebration. Their goal was to gather information about Sarah's activities and uncover any inconsistencies surrounding her alleged absence.

The news article titled 'St. Patrick's Day: A Spectacular Evening of Art and Celebration' painted a vivid picture of the grand opening gala event. Olivia read aloud, a smile playing on her lips. "The art world gathered in a glittering affair. Esteemed members, patrons, and enthusiasts witnessed this cultural milestone."

Continuing to read, Olivia's excitement grew. "Sarah's coastal landscapes stood out among the captivating pieces. They captured the essence of the shore in breathtaking detail. Her work made quite an impression."

Lily's eyes gleamed with imagination. "I can almost see it—the vibrant atmosphere, the creative energy. It must have been inspiring."

"The article also mentioned the work put in by the local art students for the soft opening on March 1st, to get the gallery open and have everything ready for the gala. The employees celebrated with a luau at the harbor. I an imagine the tropical air and hear the laughter along the shoreline."

Olivia nodded, captivated by the article. "Artists, students, and families gathered for camaraderie and creative exchange. It was a true celebration of art and community."

Their focus shifted to tracking down the people mentioned by the reporter. Armed with the list of names, Olivia and Lily aimed to gather firsthand accounts and untangle the mystery surrounding Sarah's absence.

"This article will guide us," Olivia declared, determination shining in her eyes. "We need to speak to those who were there, piece together their recollections, and uncover any inconsistencies."

Lily nodded, ready for the task at hand. "Through these firsthand accounts, we can unravel the truth and shed light on Sarah's activities."

With the news article as their compass, Olivia and Lily embarked on their mission. The echoes of that spectacular evening fueled their determination to uncover hidden truths and bring clarity to Sarah's mysterious circumstances.

Their first interviewee was Emma Turner, a talented artist and former student of Sarah's. They met at a cozy café, where Emma eagerly shared her memories of the luau and her last interaction with Sarah.

Emma's eyes sparkled with nostalgia and sadness. "The beach party was magical. We celebrated the gallery opening and Sarah's achievements. She was radiant, spreading her contagious energy."

Olivia inquired, "Did you see or hear from Sarah after the luau? We're trying to piece together her movements."

Emma's expression faltered briefly. "No, that was the last time. I reached out, but got no response. Mr. Nels mentioned her sick mother, and she needed to care for her."

Olivia and Lily exchanged a glance, noticing the consistency in the sick mother story. They thanked Emma, assuring her of their determination to find the truth.

Their next interview was with David Andrews, another artist present at the celebration. They visited his studio, filled with vibrant canvases and the scent of oil paints. As they discussed that memorable night, David's eyes sparkled with enthusiasm.

"The luau was incredible," David recalled with a grin. "Sarah had a gift for bringing people together. We celebrated her talent and the possibilities. This was a great opportunity for her and us."

Lily probed gently. "After the beach party, did you have any contact with Sarah?"

David's expression turned somber. "No, that was the last time. I tried reaching out, but there was no response. Mr. Nels mentioned her mother's illness. Doesn't make sense, and we never heard from Sarah again."

Olivia and Lily were about to leave when Olivia's eyes widened. She spotted rectangular crates secured with a vibrant red-orange string. Her heart skipped a beat. The string looked just like the one found on Jane Doe's ankle—the same unique pattern they had analyzed. Curiosity and fear surged through Olivia as she gathered the courage to ask David about it.

"Those crates over there... The string you used to secure them. Where did you get it?"

David's eyes sparkled as he led Olivia towards the crates. "Ah, keen eye! Got it from leftover gallery supplies. Mr. Nels insisted on specially manufactured rope to prevent 'substandard securing.'"

Olivia's mind raced. The distinct rope, Mr. Nels' secretive nature—it all fit. She pressed further.

"Anything else unusual about Mr. Nels or the gallery?"

David paused, eyes darting around. "He was aloof and hard to deal with. A know-it-all. A strange guy."

The puzzle pieces aligned. Olivia had to proceed with caution. She thanked David, determined to uncover the truth.

Olivia and Lily left, the weight of their discoveries heavy. The evidence mounted, driving them closer to the truth.

Next, they interviewed Jacob Reynolds, hoping for more insights.

"You're the investigators, right? About Sarah?" Jacob asked, curiosity and apprehension evident.

Olivia nodded, offering a warm smile. "That's us. Care to share your memories of the party and any interactions with Sarah?"

Jacob's gaze drifted, lost in recollection. "Man, she was a great teacher. The gallery was incredible. The luau was so much fun and Sarah shone. Last time we saw her."

Lily probed further. "Any contact with Sarah after the party?"

Jacob's expression turned grave. "Nope, not a one. Calls went unanswered. Mr. Nels mentioned her sick mom, but who knows. All I know is we never saw or heard from her again."

They thanked Jacob and headed off.

Olivia and Lily's suspicions grew. The consistent sick mom story, Mr. Nels' involvement—it felt like a smokescreen. They knew they had to dig deeper.

"Lily, something's off," Olivia whispered, brows furrowed. "It's a cover-up. We need more evidence."

Lily nodded, resolute. "Agreed, Liv. We'll untangle the web of lies."

Olivia and Lily pushed forward, gathering puzzle pieces, shedding light on the truth. Justice for Sarah was within reach.

Chapter 16
Fizz And Fuzz

Olivia and Lily hurried to the police department the next morning, their hearts pounding with anticipation and urgency. They were bursting to spill the beans to Detective Thomas about Margaret Whitman, Thomas Morrison, Mr. Nels, and the discoveries they had made from their interviews with Sarah's colleagues and students. It was time to reveal the discrepancies they had uncovered.

As they entered the detective's office, chaos greeted them—papers scattered all over, crime scene photos adorning the walls. "Well, well, well, look who's here," Detective Thomas greeted them, his eyes a mix of curiosity and skepticism. He motioned them into a cramped conference room where Lieutenant Jones was waiting, his expression stern. "Alright, ladies, let's cut to the chase. Tell me everything you've found."

Taking a deep breath, Olivia started dishing the dirt on their investigation since they identified Sarah as the mysterious Jane Doe. She filled them in on their meticulous research, their interviews with Margaret, Mr. Nels, the workers, and the artists who attended the beach party. Once she finished, she leaned back, waiting to see if their findings would be taken seriously.

Lily joined in, her voice firm and determined. "Detective Thomas, we've been talking to multiple witnesses, and guess what? Every single one of them independently mentioned seeing Sarah at the beach party.

But here's the kicker—Mr. Nels kept spinning a tale about Sarah taking care of her sick mother and being present at the gallery gala. It doesn't add up, Detective. Something's fishy here."

Detective Thomas leaned forward, his interest piqued. "Alright, fill me in on these discrepancies. What's got you all worked up?"

Olivia took a moment to gather her thoughts, then delivered her revelation with conviction. "Detective, the witnesses' accounts all align—they saw Sarah at the beach party. But here's the juicy tid-bit—Avery Randolph, who was supposed to meet Sarah, confirmed that she stood him up on his birthday, March 6th. He never heard from her again. And guess what Nels said? That she was working in the gallery on that very same day. Smells like trouble, doesn't it?"

Lily chimed in, her voice laced with sass. "Detective Thomas, there's more. When we interviewed artist David Andrews, we noticed some-thing suspicious—a peculiar red rope. Turns out, it was custom-made for Mr. Nels' shipping needs. Talk about shady business!"

Detective Thomas sat back, rubbing his chin thoughtfully. "Well, well, well, ladies. It seems like you've stirred up a hornet's nest. This case is getting hotter by the minute."

Just then, Olivia's phone buzzed. It was Patricia Morelli, and with Lieutenant Jones' approval, Olivia put her on speakerphone.

Patricia's voice crackled with urgency. "Olivia, I'm sorry for being out of touch. Just got back and heard about your investigation. How can I assist?"

Olivia gave an overview to Patricia, explaining their suspicions and the revelations from the beach party. Patricia gasped, her voice filled with intrigue. "Oh my, I left before the beach bash, but I do remem-ber Sarah mentioning something odd about certain paintings. She thought they looked fake. I didn't pay much attention back then, but now it all makes sense."

Olivia's heart raced. This was the confirmation they needed. "Patricia, if you find any notes or details that could help, it would be a game-changer. We're thirsty for the truth, and we won't rest until we find it."

With the call wrapped up, Lieutenant Jones stood up, his expression serious. "Olivia, Lily, you've given us some great leads. We'll launch an official investigation, starting with Nels and those questionable paintings. We owe it to Sarah and everyone involved to get to the bottom of this."

Olivia and Lily exchanged triumphant smiles. They had shaken things up, and now the authorities were paying attention. A new chapter of the investigation had begun, and they were ready on stand-by until justice was served.

Detective Thomas, his face determined, added, "Ladies, your sleuthing skills have impressed me. We'll leave no stone unturned in this case. I'll assemble a team, reevaluate Nels' credibility, and gather more statements from the witnesses. The truth will be revealed, mark my words."

Olivia and Lily left the police department, feeling like they had stirred a whirlwind. They were satisfied but knew there was more brewing beneath the surface. The truth was coming out, and they were determined to savor every moment.

While they had gone back home to keep up with their other cases, over the next few weeks, Olivia and Lily maintained close contact with Detective Thomas. They shared any new leads or tantalizing tidbits that crossed their path, trusting in his expertise to brew the investigation further.

Nearly three weeks later, Olivia's phone buzzed with a call from Detective Thomas. They were ready to make an arrest, and they wanted

Olivia and Lily there. The justice was about to arrive, and they were the honored guests.

Excitement coursed through Olivia and Lily's veins as they prepared for the next phase. The moment of truth was near, and they were ready to witness it.

Chapter 17
It's All Relative

O livia and Lily rushed back into town, their hearts pounding with anticipation as they met with Lieutenant Jones and Detective Thomas at the police station. The air crackled with tension, ready to reveal the shocking truth they had uncovered about Mr. Nels.

Sitting across from Detective Thomas and Lieutenant Jones, Olivia and Lilly wore expressions of excitement and apprehension. They had no idea what they were about to hear.

Lieutenant Jones leaned in, his voice tinged with incredulity. "Olivia, Lily, you won't believe it. The background check on Mr. Nels came up empty. Like he wasn't on the Earth before 1960."

Olivia's eyes widened, her mind racing to process the revelation. "So, what does that mean, he doesn't exist? I don't get it."

Lieutenant Jones nodded with a solemn expression. "Exactly. Our investigation led us to some discreet evidence gathering, and guess what we found? Mr. Nels is actually Richard Goebel, an art forger who pulled off some major cons in England."

Lily gasped, her hand flying to her mouth in shock. "Richard Goebel? The infamous art forger? What was he doing hiding in Harborville?"

Detective Thomas interjected, his voice firm with determination. "It seems Goebel wanted to escape his criminal past, start fresh, and fool everyone in the art world. He chose Harborville as his sanctuary, operating under the guise of Mr. Nels, the respected gallery owner."

Lieutenant Jones added, "But that's not all. There's another twist to this tale." He proceeded to tell Olivia and Lily about their visit to Avery Randolph, the painting, and their collaboration with the FBI's art forgery team.

Days later, they were back in the same spots, anxiously awaited the results of the FBI's evaluation. The findings would have far-reaching implications and shed light on the depths of Goebel's deceit.

Olivia, her eyes fixed on Lieutenant Jones, couldn't contain her anticipation any longer. "Lieutenant, what did the FBI say? Is the painting a forgery?"

Lieutenant Jones sighed, disappointment weighing on his voice. "I'm afraid so, Olivia. The experts examined it thoroughly, and there's no doubt about it. 'What Lies Beneath' is a counterfeit."

Olivia's heart sank, the truth landing heavily upon her. The treasured artwork turned out to be nothing but a sham, a product of Goebel's deception. She shook her head, unable to fathom the extent of his manipulation. "How could he fool everyone like that? To manipulate the art world for his own gain."

Lilly added solemnly, "Sarah must have figured it out and was going to tell Mr. Randolph."

Lieutenant Jones nodded, his frustration palpable. "Indeed, Olivia. This revelation strengthens our case against Richard Goebel. We're closing in on him, step by step."

Olivia's voice quivered with a mix of anger and determination. "We need to let Margaret, Thomas, and Robert know about this. They deserve to hear the truth about Sarah and the man responsible for her disappearance."

Detective Thomas agreed, his tone resolute. "You're right. They need to be informed, and we'll be there to support them every step of the way."

Olivia and Lily understood the weight of the situation. Their pursuit of justice for Sarah Whitman had uncovered a web of deceit, an art forger hiding in plain sight. Armed with the truth and the unwavering support of the police, they were determined to bring closure to Sarah's family and ensure that Richard Goebel faced the consequences of his actions.

Later that week, Olivia, Lily, and Detective Thomas gathered Margaret Whitman, Thomas Morrison, and Robert Reynolds in a private meeting room at the police station. The atmosphere crackled with tension as they prepared to share the shocking revelations that would reshape their understanding of Sarah's disappearance and her connection to each of them.

Detective Thomas began the meeting, his voice steady yet compassionate. "Thank you all for being here. We've made significant progress in our investigation into Sarah's case, and what we've discovered is nothing short of astounding."

Margaret, Thomas, and Robert exchanged glances, their eyes filled with a mix of curiosity and apprehension. They had no idea what was about to be revealed.

Detective Thomas continued, "Through extensive DNA analysis, we have confirmed that Sarah Whitman is the Jane Doe found in 1961. Margaret, I'm so sorry for your loss."

Margaret, her voice trembling, whispered, "Sarah... my poor sister..." Tears streamed down her face, mingling with a mix of grief and newfound understanding. "I don't understand."

"Well, here's where it gets even more unexpected. The DNA results show that Sarah is not only related to Margaret, but also to Thomas and Robert."

The room fell into stunned silence. Margaret's eyes widened, as she brought a hand to her mouth. Thomas and Robert exchanged incredulous looks, struggling to process the revelation. Detective Thomas motioned to Olivia.

She explained further, "There is no easy way to say this. The DNA indicates that Sarah is your half-sister Margaret's and also yours Thomas. It appears Margaret that your mother, Catherine, had a relationship with Thomas' father John, leading to the connection between all of you."

Lieutenant Jones, no stranger to delivering difficult news, spoke gently, "I understand this is a lot to take in. We are deeply sorry for your loss and the upheaval this revelation brings. We are here to support you and provide any answers we can."

Olivia spoke up, her voice filled with empathy. "I've been through this DNA stuff myself when I found out I wasn't who I thought I was. I'm here for you and can explain more in detail if you are open to it. Right now, we need to find out what truly happened to Sarah. We owe it to her memory and your family."

Detective Thomas nodded, his expression reflecting their shared determination. "You have our commitment. We will continue our investigation, delve deeper into the circumstances surrounding Sarah's disappearance, and seek justice. We just ask for your trust and patience as we move forward."

Margaret, Thomas, and Robert, still grappling with the shock of the revelations, agreed to cooperate and provide further assistance. They would do whatever it took to uncover the truth and bring closure to their family.

As the meeting concluded, Olivia, Lily, and Detective Thomas assured Margaret, Thomas, and Robert that they would be kept informed of any progress in the investigation. They knew the road ahead would be challenging, but their shared determination and unwavering support would guide them through.

Leaving the police station, Olivia and Lily felt the weight of their mission. The pursuit of justice had taken an unexpected turn, revealing a web of deceit and a path toward the truth. They were more determined than ever to uncover the whole story, no matter how elusive it may be.

Chapter 18
The Unveiling

O livia and Lilly were back in Harborville again after weeks away. They had gathered evidence and shared their findings with the police before leaving town. In their absence, the police had reviewed everything, conducted follow-up interviews, and built a strong case to arrest the killer of Jane Doe, or rather, Sarah Whitman.

Now, they were ready to execute their plan—a plan to expose the guilty party, reveal vital information, and ensure a swift arrest. The tension in the community room was palpable. The crowd knew they were about to hear a major announcement related to the Jane Doe case, but they had no idea the arrest would take place that night. Olivia knew the importance of having everything in order, even though she wasn't a cop anymore. Danger was always a possibility.

Olivia moved to the center of the gallery, her gaze sweeping across the room. The police, strategically positioned nearby, listened intently as she began to address the crowd. Lilly stood beside her, exuding confidence and determination. Olivia took a deep breath and projected her voice with authority.

"Ladies and gentlemen, thank you all for being here today. I stand before you to reveal the truth, to shine a light on the mystery that has haunted our community for too long. Through genetic genealogy and extensive research, we have uncovered the identity of our Jane

Doe. She is none other than Sarah Whitman, a beloved member of our town."

The room buzzed with anticipation as Olivia continued, captivating the audience with carefully chosen words. "Our journey began with a simple desire for closure, to identify the woman found on our shores. We embarked on an investigation, tracing family trees, uncovering connections, and relying on the power of DNA."

Lilly stepped forward, her voice strong and resolute. "Through cutting-edge techniques and meticulous analysis, we identified shared genetic markers between our Jane Doe and members of the Whitman, Morrison, and Reynolds families. Science has confirmed that Sarah Whitman, the talented artist, is our beloved Jane Doe."

Gasps and whispers filled the room. Shock and relief mingled among the crowd. The community had mourned Sarah's loss, and now they faced the reality of her fate.

Empowered by the audience's reactions, Olivia continued her presentation. "But our work is not done. We believe there is more to Sarah's disappearance than meets the eye. Inconsistencies, discrepancies, and suspicious behavior have led us to suspect foul play."

Eyes darted around the room, the audience exchanging glances as they realized the depth of the investigation.

Olivia's voice grew stronger, her resolve unwavering. "The police have worked tirelessly with us, and together, we will bring those responsible to justice. Our community deserves closure, and we will not rest until the truth is revealed."

Applause and murmurs of support filled the room. The people of Harborville stood united, determined to uncover the secrets that had plagued their town for too long.

Olivia stepped aside, allowing Chief Blackwood to take the floor. The room fell into a hushed silence as the chief cleared his throat and began his address. His commanding voice demanded attention as he began to describe the details of the investigation.

"Ladies and gentlemen, thank you for being here. As Olivia mentioned, we have worked closely with her and Lilly to unravel the mysteries surrounding Sarah Whitman's disappearance. Our dedicated investigators have left no stone unturned."

Chief Blackwood paused, scanning the room, ensuring he had everyone's full attention. "During our investigation, we followed every lead, delving into every aspect of Sarah's life. It is with great regret that I must inform you that the astonishing 'What Lies Beneath' painting purchased by Mr. Randolph has been proven to be a forgery."

A collective gasp swept through the room. Shock and disbelief hung in the air as the audience grappled with the revelation.

Chief Blackwood continued, his voice steady. "Our forgery investigation has exposed a web of deceit and manipulation surrounding Sarah's work at the gallery. We have reason to believe that Mr. Jacob Nels, her boss, was involved in a scheme to pass off counterfeit artwork as authentic masterpieces."

Outrage and astonishment filled the room. People exchanged incredulous glances, unable to reconcile their image of the respected gallery owner with the reality of his involvement in such a nefarious scheme.

Chief Blackwood pressed on, his tone resolute. "Through forensic analysis and interviews, we have uncovered evidence linking Mr. Nels to the forgery operation. Search warrants have been executed, revealing a hidden workshop where counterfeit paintings were being created. Mr. Nels is currently under arrest."

A murmur of disbelief swept through the room. The audience struggled to process the depth of the deception that had unfolded within their close-knit art community.

"As we speak, our officers are collecting crucial evidence to build a solid case against Mr. Nels and anyone else involved in this forgery operation. Justice will prevail, and those responsible for Sarah's disappearance and the forgery scheme will face the consequences."

The room fell into a heavy silence. The weight of Chief Blackwood's words settled upon the audience, and they knew that their community was forever changed. The pursuit of truth and justice had become their collective mission.

In the days that followed, news of the art world scandal and the arrest of Jacob Nels spread like wildfire. The community grappled with the revelations, seeking to rebuild trust and restore integrity. Olivia and Lilly received praise for their tireless dedication and collaboration with the police, their unwavering pursuit of justice serving as an example to others. Sarah's memory was honored, her tragic fate finally finding a resolution.

As the process unfolded, the people of Harborville rallied together, united in their pursuit of justice for Sarah Whitman and a renewed commitment to preserving the integrity and authenticity of the art that had once brought them together. The truth would prevail, and the community would heal, forever changed by the resilience and unwavering determination of those who sought to uncover the hidden truths that lay beneath the surface of their idyllic town.

As Olivia and Lilly headed home, they sat across from each other on the plane, their faces etched with a mixture of exhaustion and triumph. Now, as they reflected on their accomplishments, they engaged in a conversation that encapsulated their journey.

Olivia smiled, her eyes shining with satisfaction. "Lilly, can you believe it? We did it. We identified Sarah and brought closure to the police, her family, and our community."

Lilly's voice trembled, "I'm still in awe, Olivia. We worked tirelessly on this case, and to see it come to fruition, to know that we made a real difference—it's beyond rewarding."

Olivia nodded, her voice filled with pride and relief. "Absolutely. We uncovered the truth behind Sarah's identity, shed light on her family connections, and helped bring closure to her loved ones. Our work has made an impact that will last."

Lilly's eyes gleamed with a renewed sense of purpose. "And let's not forget the impact on the community. By bringing this criminal to justice, we've made residents feel safer, reminding them that justice prevails."

Olivia nodded, her voice tinged with determination. "Our mission goes beyond solving cases. It's about making a lasting impact, about ensuring that every unidentified victim receives the justice they deserve. We've given Sarah her name back and provided closure to her family, allowing them to heal and remember her as she truly was."

Lilly reached out, her hand gently resting on Olivia's. "You're right, Olivia. Our dedication, our research, it was all worth it. Sarah's case is proof that perseverance can make a difference. We won't stop here; there are more mysteries to unravel, more lives to bring closure to."

"Yes, Lilly, new cases to work, new books to write and new podcast episodes to record!"

They sat there, in a shared moment of reflection, their journey coming full circle. As they celebrated their achievements, Olivia and Lilly found strength in each other. From their own personal DNA drama, they emerged with a mission—a mission to make a difference, to seek justice for the forgotten and the voiceless.

The End

Afterword

Thank you for purchasing and reading this book. It is important to me in so many ways.

More importantly it's important to the **over 14,400 unidentified humans** that remain in morgues and unmarked graves across the United States.

These are people's mothers, fathers, sisters, brothers, and children.

They may be victims of crimes or just left his earth and remain nameless.

I aim to change that.

It's scary to write, publish and put it all out there but I couldn't go on without doing *something* for these poor people.

I created these books to raise awareness of these cases – this book inspired by one.

The Unknown Humans Remain podcast does exist, another avenue to spread the word.

For more information and to join us in the initiative, please register for our newsletter:

https://dashboard.mailerlite.com/forms/445024/906231401225
93073/share

Last but not least, please consider leaving a helpful review on Amazon letting me know what you thought of the book.

Thank you!

Christine

New Releases

A Cozy Mystery Series Featuring Private Investigator Nikki Hunt

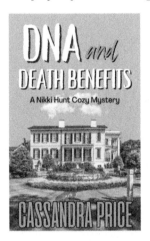

Get Your Copy Now

In the hallowed halls of an esteemed law firm, a shocking crime disrupts the tranquility that once prevailed.

This tale of deception and intrigue blends the enigmatic world of legal professionals with an enthralling whodunit.

Join Nikki Hunt as she untangles the dark secrets that lie at the heart of a murder, risking everything in a race against time where trust is a rare commodity and danger lurks in every shadow.

https://www.amazon.com/dp/B0C9P56PVJ

Printed in Great Britain
by Amazon

26637865R00067